Sallie Neill Roach

Theon

A tale of the American civil war

Sallie Neill Roach

Theon
A tale of the American civil war

ISBN/EAN: 9783337174231

Printed in Europe, USA, Canada, Australia, Japan

Cover: Foto ©Andreas Hilbeck / pixelio.de

More available books at **www.hansebooks.com**

A TALE OF THE AMERICAN CIVIL WAR.

BY

SALLIE NEILL ROACH.

"NO CROSS, NO CROWN."

PHILADELPHIA:
J. B. LIPPINCOTT & CO.
1882.

TO

THE LOST CAUSE,

TO THE COMFORT OF ITS BEREAVED ONES,

TO THE MEMORY OF ITS DEAD,

TO THE HONOR OF ITS SURVIVORS,

THIS VOLUME

IS DEDICATED.

THEON.

CANTO FIRST.

I.

MAUD RUTHERFORD'S JOURNAL.

" *He* came this evening ;—to-morrow, *we* go.
Ever thus has it been ; here and there, to and 'fro,
Our pathways have wandered, yet never once met.
Have the changes of years taught his heart to forget ?
Forget!   I have revelled where Pleasure held sway ;
I have laughed, sung, and danced, and the world calls me
  gay ;
I have reigned over hearts,—yet in each silent hour
That memory comes with its maddening power.
It is love, crushed and dead,—turned in mockery to hate ;
And it floats o'er my path like a grim-visaged fate."

II.

THEON.

Still writing ?   Excuse me.   We are waiting for you.
The moonlight is lovely :—enchanting the view.
Why, cousin ! how pale !   Are you ill ?

MAUD.

Not at all.

Only weary, Theon.

THEON.

Will you go to the ball?

MAUD.

Perhaps.

THEON.

I entreat you, then, come for this walk.
The air is refreshing;—a good social talk
Will rally your spirits and banish the blues.
Come! Uncle is waiting;—you must not refuse;—
He is on the piazza.

MAUD.   .

In company?

THEON.

No:

Alone, and impatient.

MAUD.

At once I will go.

III.

Draping her shawl with a rare, queenly grace,
And banishing each sign of grief from her face,
She followed Theon, and her secret was hushed,
And the dark, haunting memory silently crushed.

IV.

Niagara by moonlight. The mad torrent roars
And leaps o'er the rough rocks above, till it pours
Its mighty strength out, in one wild fearful leap,
Then surges and groans in the terrible deep.

Floating above, like some pale phantom shroud,
Half lingering, half flying, the fleecy mist-cloud.
The moonbeams have clothed it with soft silver light,
While the torrent, subdued, pays its homage to night.

V.

Together the cousins gazed out on the stream
In mute admiration. The moon's fairy gleam
Fell full o'er Theon, thus revealing her face,
Expressive in earnestness, crowned with the grace
Of pure, happy womanhood, ere the dark leaf
Had been turned that would give for life's sunshine life's
      grief.
Her soul drank the scene with a rapture that thrilled
And awed her to silence. The dark eyes were filled,
And her breathing came quick, as the picture she drew
By light elfin touch floated past to her view.

VI.

In the face of her cousin, half turned, there was told
A spirit defiant, and haughty, and cold.
Yet one could but mark in the quick, restless glance
A craving unfed.

MAUD.

      This is Nature's romance.
Such is life's mockery: fragile and fair
As the beautiful mist, hov'ring soft in the air,
Brightest hopes float around, and yet, one look below
Reveals the abyss where the mad waters flow;
And the visions we love pass away on the cloud,
While yet others come,—weaving each its own shroud.

VII.

Quickly answered Theon:

> "There undoubtedly lives
In each heart a motive, an impulse that gives
To life a reality.   Is this in vain?
Each emotion a dream? every craving a pain?"

MAUD.

You are meeting the world.   But a year or two since
I trusted life's promise.   Time served to convince
Myself of the error, and holds to my view
But hollowness where I had thought all was true.
Man meets with his fellows,—is courteous and sad
As occasion requires; ofttimes smiles and is glad;
Yet far 'neath the mask that he wears to the world
Lies a heart drifting, trustless,—its mockery hurled
By the throng in his face.   Borne along on the tide
Of the fate-impelled stream does his good impulse glide;
And nothing is left that is steadfast and pure,
No friendship to strengthen,—no love to endure.

VIII.

THEON.

Hark! the roar of the waters!   Yon torrent, whose glory
Man e'er loves to yield, strives to tell its wild story;*—
A tale of devotion, unswerving, and true;
A legend, perchance, and yet holding in view
The heart's full fidelity.   Years long since dead,
Ere the white man had come, knew the red warrior's tread,
As he roamed unrestrained through his own forest land;
And pilgrimage brought to this wild spot some band.

---

* Guide-Book.

Came yearly a night when their council-fires burned,
And the face of each brave was to yon torrent turned;
For the lot must be cast on that night to decide
Which maiden is fairest and fittest to guide
O'er the rocks where the water in mad fury falls,
The tribe's yearly gift to the Spirit who calls!
This evening, methought that the maidens I saw,
Assembled in waiting,—their lips sealed with awe;
For this honor, the greatest their tribe can bestow,
Must hurl the fair guide to the dread depths below.
In silence the last lot is drawn, and of all,
The fairest one there has received the low call.
'Tis the stern chieftain's daughter, his idol in life,
The one living being whose voice, from the strife
Which means to him honor, falls soft on his ear,
And wooes him to peace and a love that is dear.
Father and daughter together have heard
The time-honored summons. A chief may be stirred
By no tender feelings. The maiden descends
From a long line of warriors, and meekly she bends
To the law of her tribe. Perchance e'en as now
The moonlight fell soft over leaflet and bough,
And poured its pure rays on yon turbulent wave,
So soon to bear youth to its terrible grave.
From the edge of yon isle, fancy paints to my view,
Floating out on the tide, a white, tiny canoe,
Full laden with flowers and fruits ripe and rare,
And in it a maiden, in robes pure and fair,
As if for her bridal dressed. Calmly she guides
The boat to the breakers, and silently rides
To her martyr-like doom. No pausing, no fear;
No last, lingering look; neither murmur nor tear;

Though the moon that we love pictures bright the dread
　　　verge,
And the mad rapids chant (hear it now!) the last dirge!
But a loud cry is heard, for another boat speeds
On its way through the rapids. The mariner heeds
Nor shouts of his people, nor look of distress
That the maiden bestows. The warrior's redress
From his forefathers' laws is asserted by love :
E'en the Indian, while stifling his sorrow, may prove
His life's sole devotion. They reach yonder brink,
Exchange one intense look of love, and then sink
With the force of the plunge in abysses below,
And father and daughter have shared the death-throe!

IX.

Theon's voice hushed, and her tender eyes glistened.
Her hearers had watched her bright face while they listened ;
And they read there illumed by the fervor of youth
Her earnest devotion,—her reverence for truth.
The legend was more to her, far, than a story ;
It bore to her mind all the grandeur and glory
Of man's power to love. They had felt as she spoke.
This one thought was uppermost. Maud, at last, broke
The quiet that reigned.

X.

MAUD.

　　　　For an idolized child,
A father, perchance, may have been rash and wild,
When maddened by grief. 'Tis the one lasting love ;
The only, I ween, that, when full tried, may prove
Unselfish and true.

Said her uncle :

"What, then,

Of love that is pledged between women and men ?
Have you no faith in the bride's holy vow ?
No trust in true manhood ? no impulse to bow
To that peerless devotion, that love all divine,
Which legend and verse yield the heart's sacred shrine ?"

XI.

She answered him coldly :

"'Tis well to rehearse

A tried, faithful love : 'tis the language of verse ;
But life has another. Its fitful romance
Is worn down and wearied, and hearts must advance :
They pass from one love to another to find
Each new one has left its excitement behind.
Much that is given to Love's fabled name
Is born in man's greater desire for fame.
And oft, were Ambition and Love face to face,
Ambition would triumph,—bid Love yield it place !"

XII.

Her uncle was startled ; each fierce, bitter word
Came strangely from one who as yet had ne'er heard
Other words than were pleasing. On him seemed the
        years
To have borne with a weight, and their clouds and their
        tears
Had left dismal traces. With quick, eager look
He scanned the fair face, which, a closely-sealed book,
No secrets betrayed. But his own face grew pale
And his full brow contracted, as if the dark trail
Of some memory crossed him.

XIII.

Theon looked aghast.
"O Maud!" she exclaimed, "when the bright years are
　　　past,—
The years of our youth, when we do, think, and feel
All that clothes an old age with its woe or its weal;
If the words you have spoken must prove themselves true,
And the years shall but serve all our weal to undo;
If life is a mockery, ties quickly broken,
And pledges but hollow, that seem fair when spoken;
If time brings it thus, it were better that youth
Should lay itself down in the grave of its truth!
No! Love is eternal, Ambition is mortal;
And, sooner or later, must reach the closed portal,
Before which it falls in its dire helplessness,
While its harvest shall yield it but bitter distress."

MAUD.

You speak with an earnestness rare for your years.
Have you learned the full meaning of love? Cease your fears!
Time has turned me a page. Love may promise, but reaps
A desolate harvest. A strange passion keeps
Its sway over hearts. Woman reigns their known queen;
And each has her votaries flitting between
The present and past. Woman triumphs to crush,
And phantom hopes beckon us on.

XIV.

THEON.

　　　　　Cousin! Hush!
For shame for those words! For to woman 'tis given
To cherish most sacred that dear gift of Heaven.

'Tis her duty to guard it, and shield it, and keep
Love's light burning bright, where the darkness lies deep.
In my girlhood I paused and with reverence heard,
And reverently uttered that talisman word.
While I know not its meaning, yet, reverently now,
There is that in my heart to its presence will bow.
Though its mysteries hidden lie far from my view,
There is that in my nature asserts it is true;
And my whole spirit bends to this unexplained love,
And yields it the homage due truth from above.

XV.

" Bravely spoken, my darling!" Clyde Rutherford cried.
" Be those words your life's motto, that spirit your pride!
See, the park is deserted, and soft music falls
On the quiet of night, and to revelry calls.
Companions await. Maud, a young friend of mine
Will meet us to-night. Must he bow to the shrine
Of your phantom?"
                        Said she:
                                " Time will prove; we'll away."
He answered her, slowly:
                                " Time proves, and for aye."

CANTO SECOND.

I.

A BRIGHT-LIGHTED parlor, where Queen Pleasure dwells,
And sweet, tender melody lingers, and swells,
And floats on the air, where its soft echoed hush
Still renders more fearful the rapids' mad rush.
Beauty is there in its unrivalled power,
And lends its full charm to each quick-fleeting hour;
Light feet trip merrily on in the dance;
Anon, joyous greetings the pleasures enhance.

II.

But Maud here is missing.   The long-assumed air,
And quick, sparkling laugh, hiding traces of care,
For one time have failed her.   Unable to meet
The man she had loved, she has chosen retreat
From the world to her chamber.   For, reaching far back
Past the scenes and the changes that crowd in the track
Of a few fleeting years, she has lived once again
Her beautiful dream.   But, alas! now the pain
That followed its brightness has deep sunken down,
And its wild throbs of anguish seem ever the frown
That shades her young life.

III.

                    In the years that were past,
The lot of her parents abroad had been cast.

14

Yet the preference and usage in early years gained,
Unaltered by distance or time, were retained.
Their daughter, imbibing that love of romance,
And sparkling vivacity native to France,
Was granted that freedom of action we see
With Americans only.   Chaperoned and yet free,
Her light restraint placed not in utter defiance
The high social custom : yet taught that reliance
On self, maidens learn, when permitted to use
Individual judgment, their future to choose.
Thus it came, at the time when the young girl first feels
The heart of a woman ; when instinct reveals
A nature expanding,—a mind knowing higher
And nobler emotions, which thrill and inspire ;
At her feet there was laid, as an offering pure,
A rich, manly love, having strength to endure.
But the wakened emotion was scarcely in flame
Ere smothered by one wearing statelier name.
It was not enough she should know herself loved,—
That love must be tested, its ardor be proved.
Hence the lover was spurned with indifferent air,
And the days rolled along.   Though no traces of care
Were seen in Maud's face, yet her young heart grew
      cold,
And hardened, and bitter, and seared, like the old
Forest leaf when it falls.   Imperious, still,
Her fault was unseen : but defiant, her will
Condemned to the grave every once cherished trust,
And mocked at the love that her folly made dust.
Turning for respite again to the world,
She launched on society's wave, and was hurled
Here and there by the tide ; and her smouldered desire
For love, burning on in unquenchable fire,

Seemed now but the craving for homage. High place
Was given the proud, social queen. Yet that face—
The one face of all, that had wielded such power
O'er the tale of her life—never had, till that hour,
Again crossed her path. But to-night it has risen
Like some silent spectre escaped from the prison
Where a dead past had doomed it, and bursting control,
Her long-smothered passion has swept o'er her soul.
She dare not confront it ! One touch of *his* hand,
One glance of *his* eye, she would lose her command.
Had his love been enduring, the test that she craved
Had provoked perseverance,—her heart had been saved.
But to-night there was merriment dwelt in his eye,
And she felt, could the past be recalled, no reply
Would come from his heart e'en as one brief regret.
Could that love be true that could love and forget ?
Perchance it might be, as the weary years rolled,
Another would hear the same words that he told
So gently to her ; and another be glad,
E'en as she had once been. Ah ! the thought made her
        mad :
It burned in her brain, and it rankled her heart,
And pierced her soul through like some keen, fiery dart.
'Twas love that she trifled with,—love she defied,
Whose embers the ashes of years could not hide.

IV.

A riddle is woman. Of what rank or nation,
There exists in her mind, by instinctive creation,
An ardent desire to reign. Not by might,—
Such power were worthless. She craves as her right
A full homage given, and loyally kept.
Was it not even this, when the old serpent crept

In the garden and won Mother Eve, that did move
Her to tempt and win Adam? Would he for her love
Do this thing? And he did. Woman rarely commands
By imperious sway; for her delicate hands
Are too slight and weak the strong sceptre to wield;
She guides it unseen, yet the power it may yield
Is none the less sweet. Woman speaks to the soul,
And wakens emotions to feel her control,
While man bends submissive. This instinct is given
In kindness to her by a wise, tender Heaven.
It is not alone the demand of Ambition;
That woman has lived in most royal position,
Even ruling a nation, who turned from it all,
From the glitter and pomp of display to this call
Of her heart; 'neath its sway tyrannized here and there
In petty caprices, forgetting the care
And grandeur of state.

V.

It means simply this:
That woman, to bask in a sunshine of bliss,
Must love,—be loved truly; for her sake alone;
Must feel herself absolute queen on her throne.
Her subject's obedience to each light desire
Proves the homage she wins; hence she prizes it higher
Than the monarch his fame. Each impulse is spent,
The tenor of life is instinctively bent,
Unconsciously oft though it be, thus to gain
What thrills her with pleasure, whose absence is pain.
Be her love true and pure, concentrated, and brought
In its trust to one heart,—then alike 'twill be fraught
With good both to woman and man; giving more,
As its value is prized, of the blessing in store;

Constantly winning an homage whose worth
O'ershadows that given all monarchs of earth.
Yet again be her craving for love undefined,
Disregarded, unhallowed, 'twill render her mind
Restless, roving, uneasy : 'twill eagerly feed
Every thought of ambition or self.   In its greed
It will roam unrestrained ; seeking no resting-place,—
Finding none,—aimlessly turn and retrace
The paths it has trodden.   This phantom Maud saw
And strove to appease.   For the grandeur and awe
Of the spirit of Love lay concealed 'neath the tomb,
Where Selfishness nourished its germ into bloom;
And gave to the woman that great sense of power
Over hearts that had proven her terrible dower;
Making thus of a blessing a curse that should haunt
Her poor aching heart in unsatisfied want.
O'er her nature untamed her imperative will,
Impelled by the longing her heart's void to fill,
Arose in defiance, and trampling on fate,
As rich treasure gathered a fierce, burning hate ;
A hate that should conquer and bring to her feet
His heart crushed and bleeding.   Revenge would be
    sweet
Could her hand sweep the strings of his life with a strain
Whose wail would re-echo her own throbbing pain.

VI.

She passed to her window, threw open the sash,
And heard o'er the roar of the mad waters' dash
The sound of the music's low ripple and trill.
As she seated herself on the broad window-sill,
The balcony swarmed with the dancers who sought
The cool air of night with renewed vigor fraught.

She watched them awhile,—and anon the low hum
Of their voices arose: then unbidden would come
The half-denied wish that she there might discern
That voice whose echoes would ever return.
She starts as she marks in the moon's mellow light,
Scarce revealed from the shadow, then merged in the
    night,
The form so well known. 'Tis the same manly face,
The same haughty carriage and dignified grace.
And with him?—Theon! She who dared to defend
Her maidenly trust in emotions that lend
New impulse to life. Could she see Theon bear
The treasure that mocked at her own heart's despair?

VII.

Theon, yet unconscious of clouds she had raised,
Was radiant and happy. The beauty all praised
Was that of pure loveliness, gently appealing
At once to the heart. It was spirit revealing
Itself in the features, and screened 'neath the veil
Of utter unconsciousness. Life wove a tale
Like pictures from dreamland, and Hope painted there
A future all brilliant, and peaceful, and fair.
Tenderly shielded and screened from its strife,
Her earliest maidenhood looked upon life
As childhood had found it. Unknown, aught but truth,
Seemed all things reflected and brightened by youth.
Never dreaming of conquest, she reigned, and was glad
That all things were happy, that nothing seemed sad.

VIII.

Her champion in childhood,—Maud's hero in scenes
That memory treasured like weird, broken dreams,

Stands near in attendance.　One reads in his face,
Decisive in outline, firm, manly in trace,
A sternness and strength, by which one is impressed
That manhood will come from life's struggle, confessed
By foemen, the victor.

IX.

　　　　　　　　Montgomery, from college,
Had started life's journey equipped well with knowledge.
With resolute will he had turned to his books,
Exploring the hidden recesses and nooks
Which Science, enticingly, scarcely reveals,
Inviting the search for the store she conceals.
In his own eager nature, he knew not a pause
Until he had mastered each precept and cause :
And he stepped out in life from the closed college-door
With that same restless longing to seek and explore ;
Yet having no purpose, save but to achieve
Whate'er he began ; nor would he receive
Aught else but a victory.　Gifted with health,
And favored by fortune with bountiful wealth,
He started as zealously now in pursuit
Of pleasure, as years since he sought for the root
Of old Latin verbs.

X.

　　　　　　　In the earliest flush
Of manhood's full prime, when his buoyant blood's rush
Impelled his emotions, he felt the first glow
Of what is called love; and every wild throe
Was greeted and nursed in the heart's bounding gladness,
Till the pleasure was pain, and the ecstasy madness.
He offered his love, and then stood back aghast,
As the treasure, when won, was aside lightly cast.

XI.

This wantonly heartless and frivolous act
Had burst on his chivalrous soul, a stern fact;
And forth from him brought upon all of the sex
The judgment and censure due one.   Not to vex
And wholly outrage his loved ideas of woman,
(Hitherto deemed more angelic than human,)
He chose not to think of the blight cast upon her,
By charging her, trusted, with full-meant dishonor;
But, rather, excused her by lack of capacity
To feel, and to cherish with steadfast tenacity,
As it were, life itself, passions grand that control
The heart of the man and burn deep in his soul.
Years had passed since that time, and yet from his seclusion,
Enveloped in self, he had nursed his delusion.
He looked upon woman as unfit to reason;
A child who will treasure each joy for a season;
By right of her own weaker nature appealing
To man for protection; yet never once feeling
A man's stronger motive that urged the world's strife,
And held name and honor far dearer than life.
The storm-burst once over, he passed on his way,
Never pausing to gather the fragments that lay
All scattered around.   So had chivalrous trust
And reverence for woman been crumbled to dust.

XII.

For the first time, to-night, since the years long ago,
When he left his young playmate, a mere boy aglow
With the bright hopes of life, he had met with that friend
And companion of boyhood.   What potence to rend

Old attachments have years!   Face to face with the world,
He had seen boyish sentiments, long cherished, hurled
One by one to the ground.   From their ruins had risen
A spirit of strength that had chafed as in prison,
'Neath customs enforced by Society's laws;
But knowing no purpose, he guessed not the cause,
Only mocked its results, and held all in derision,
And drew within self with more careful precision.
Could his boyhood's companion, by right of the dower
To a true woman given, possess now the power
To open that door that his own hands had closed,
And waken the strength that so long had reposed?

XIII.

Swiftly the hours of pleasure wore on,
And he lingered unconscious of all near Theon,
Till her uncle had bade her remember the bloom
And freshness of youth must soon perish in gloom
If much overtaxed.   Wishing, then, a " Good-night!"
He watched her light form as it passed out of sight
Like a beautiful dream.   For he knew that a spell
Her presence had wrought; how, he scarcely could tell;
Yet there rose in his heart, like the memories of youth,
A mute recognition of woman's full truth.

XIV.

The revellers passed from the room one by one;
The lights were extinguished, the pleasure task done;
The gay voices hushed, and the Spirit of Sleep
Reigned over the place.   All was still, save the deep,
Angry roar of the waters.   And yet in unrest
Two persons were thinking.   The two who expressed

Their great unbelief in Love's power to control,
And wake from both sexes, soul's answer to soul.
Two idols were shattered. The man's boasted strength
Was put to the shame. Woman's conquest at length
Had suffered defeat. And Theon, who had taught,
To each the great lesson so heavily fraught
With the issues of life, like an innocent child,
Smiled sweetly in slumber of those undefiled.
Will the beautiful angel that comes in our dreams,
To paint each bright picture of hope as it seems
To those who would read it, portray to her there
The influence she has that night brought to bear
On Montgomery and Maud? And which in its rebound
Must mark her own life? Will the echo resound
With the truth, and the good be triumphant at last,
And the error lie low in the grave of the past?

CANTO THIRD.

I.

THE day awoke beautiful, bright, and serene:
The torrent rolled on with fresh strength, and the screen
Of mist hov'ring round, was arched o'er by the light
And glittered with rainbows.   The softness of night
Had vanished before the full orient dawning
Announced the approach of the monarch of morning.

II.

Along by the torrent two gentlemen wandered
As friends holding intercourse.   One of them pondered,
Or answered to trivial remarks with the air
Of one all engrossed with some idea or care.
His listless unheeding of beauty around
Bore witness of one who, still seeking, had found
Nowhere the fulfilment of what he desired,
Nor felt by the spirit of action inspired.

III.

They had seated themselves on the low outer wall
Of the Point, near the rock where the cataracts fall,
When his friend strove to rouse him.

HASTINGS.

                          Come, Ethric, confess
The thought which this morning seems so to oppress.
24

You were joyous last evening; has one transient morrow
Cast over your life dull foreboding or sorrow?

MONTGOMERY.

There are moments in life, when, like links in a chain,
Each object reverts to some season of pain
One has known in the past.   Here I happened to think,
As we wended our way on this high dizzy brink,
And marked the mad bounding of waves in their flow,
And deep angry seething in yon pool below,
How much they resemble some treasure of youth,
By the life-current borne o'er the rock of untruth;
There gone, past recall, floats the wrecked, shapeless mass,
Drifting on with the tide to the broad ocean pass.

HASTINGS.

'Tis easy to see that the past you revive.
Am I wrong if I judge that there yet is alive
A fostered remembrance?   The lady you've seen?
I speak of Miss Rutherford.

MONTGOMERY.

I know whom you mean.
And I know she is here; but a fortunate chance
Prevented our meeting.   That shadowed romance
Had best be forgotten; its memories bring
The arrows of doubt with their poisoned sting.

HASTINGS.

You loved her, then, Ethric?

MONTGOMERY.

Yes; like the fierce flame
That burns all to ashes!—if that holy name

3

Can be given such madness. That eager flame, cherished,
E'en as it was kindled, had not, perchance, perished,
But lived to grow steady. Yet oft it is needed
The first fire of youth—rash, impetuous, unheeded—
Should burn itself out, that the full ruddy glow
Of manhood be felt. Even then there is woe,
To whom, having kindled the flame till it burn,
Then feeling its warmth, shall in mockery turn.

HASTINGS.

But, Ethric, I studied her well, and I thought
That deep in her heart was a strong chord that brought,
In response to your touch, a quick, answering, thrill;
And, mark me, it wails in a minor tone still!

MONTGOMERY.

Can that be love that can wilfully crush
The heart of another? Is love made to hush
And silently lie to be trod on, and never
Its presence betray? Love asserts itself ever.

HASTINGS.

Has this thought occurred?—that she sought but a proof
Of your earnestness; holding the rich prize aloof,
She would test your endurance?

MONTGOMERY.

          That motive is pride.
And if love existed, so low 'neath the tide
Of that current 'twas plunged, that, its purity lost,
Its wealth paid the price that such vanity cost.
True, that is prized most which is hardest to gain.
But is that worth prizing which *wills* to give pain?

HASTINGS.

What prompted her conduct?

MONTGOMERY.

That craving which since
She ever has shown,—which has served to convince
That my censure was just. 'Tis the longing to wield
A sway over hearts that shall cause each to yield
Her place as its queen. 'Tis the longing for power;
She wins to destroy, and exults in her dower.

HASTINGS.

What if you meet her?

MONTGOMERY.

'Twould be e'en as though
We had slightest acquaintance. True, memory may go
Through the back paths of years and refuse to forget.
It fosters with me just this passing regret:
I loved an ideal, of which she had seemed
The fullest embodiment. Loving, I dreamed
That women were angels, whose influence should win
Man's turbulent nature from discord and sin.
Presto!—the awakening! The mask thrown aside
Left distorted and bare what its presence could hide.
The ideal was my own. But the woman,—well! well!
Was only a woman. I grieve for the spell.
You have not met her cousin?

HASTINGS.

The débutante? No.

I saw her last evening.

MONTGOMERY.

It seems long ago,
As children we played, when the child's heart could speak
Only truth as it felt; when to wade through the creek,
Or to win in a race, was the richest known pleasure,
And a wild-flower found was esteemed a bright treasure.
I was her champion by right of my years;
Helped her over rough places, soothed grave, childish fears.
She has grown into womanhood now, and last night
I thought as we talked, what a beautiful sight
It would be could she keep through society's maze
The innocent freshness of those happy days.

HASTINGS.

Then she is not changed?

MONTGOMERY.

Oh, no! Not as yet.
She is fresh from her school-room. The fashions that fret
And freeze o'er the heart have till now just begun
To show their bright edges. Perchance ere is done
Their pitiless work, her pure soul may discover
The blight that is hid and so fair gilded over.

HASTINGS.

Your mind is embittered. You still see concealed
'Neath each pleasure a curse to be ere long revealed,
And sting with its venom. Is this the first time
You have met your old playmate?

MONTGOMERY.

Yes; touched she the chime
Of memory's bells, and sweet melodies gave

From a past that is sacred, though long in its grave.
May its influence shield her !

HASTINGS.

       All speak of her beauty.
Her face is like sunshine. May life's fulfilled duty
Leave no shadows on it ! But see through yon trees
I mark the light float of a veil on the breeze.
Miss Rutherford comes. You will meet her ? Then pray
Emerge from past shadows.

IV.

      He hastened away.
Ethric joined Theon and her uncle.

V.

ETHRIC.

      Good-morning !
You are tempted, I see, by the glorious dawning,
And come to contrast with the memory of night
The great torrent bathed in the first flood of light.

VI.

Mr. Rutherford hastened his hand to extend,
And with rare courtliness greeted his friend :
A kind warmth of manner controlled every act
Of the time-honored gentleman.

MR. RUTHERFORD.

      Early, in fact ;
But to-day we return, and this maiden of mine
Insisted once more we repair to the shrine

Of her stories and legends and have the last glance,
As the earliest sunbeams begin their swift dance
In the quiet of morning.
                    " You leave, then, to-day?"
Ethric said, quickly ; " and travel which way?"

MR. RUTHERFORD.

To the South—to our homes.   The horizon o'ercast
With dark, floating clouds, now portends the full blast
That ere long may sweep o'er our beautiful land,
And scatter its laurels of fame on the strand
Of wrecked human hopes.   I would be on the soil
That my fathers have held.   I would there wait the coil
That steadily winds,—hoping still it may break,
And the dark, lowering clouds may their harmless flight take.

MONTGOMERY.

Say you so?   Can it be, in all calmness you think
The glory we prize totters now on the brink
Of utter destruction?   Forebodings, perchance,
Have rendered you gloomy, and cast your swift glance
'Mid only the shadows of yon horoscope,
Their dark outlines screening the brightness of hope.

MR. RUTHERFORD.

It is youth that speaks thus ; but, alas! when the years
Have unrolled to your view their sharp outlines of fears,
And shown the dark side of our own human nature,
With the truth that would live crushed and stunted in
            stature ;—
When you have watched o'er each bright hope, long
            cherished,
And wept by its grave, when, alas! it has perished ;—

Perchance in that time the soft glow that is cast
From the sunbeams of youth may be thrown in the past,
And yield to the dread of experience sage,
And the shadows that come, and will lengthen with age.
I look in the distance and turn in affright
From the terrible phantoms that come to my sight;
For long columns shake the loved soil with their tread,
And countless graves mark the last rest of the dead;
While over the hillsides and plains a mad flood
Pours its full, sweeping torrent. I shrink! It is blood!

ETHRIC.

If so be, if the hope that is fostered by youth
Be blighted and crushed by the terrible truth
Which your vision portrays,—a Virginian, I pledge
My life that Virginia in true, loyal hedge
Be solemnly guarded,—her dear, sacred name
Undimmed and untarnished shall still live in fame.
I pledge her my honor, and yet with Hope's hand
I wipe out this vision of woe to the land.

MR. RUTHERFORD. ˙

Amen! Be it thus! Ere the mantle of snow
Shall again wrap the earth every true heart will know
The fate that awaits us. Let each duty learn
As each prizes honor! Child, let us return
From our long morning wandering.

ETHRIC.

Nay, lady, remain.
Permit me, sir, now to attend her. The pain
Of parting will come ere the brief morning hours

Have counted their time.   Let us walk 'neath the bowers
Of yon stately trees.

VII.

Ethric offered his arm
To Theon as her uncle turned off.   The bright charm
Of maidenly freshness seemed purer 'mid scenes
Of nature's own wildness than when, 'neath the gleams
Of light in the ball-room, it won him apart
From the many whose polished excuses for heart
Had grown so monotonous.

VIII.

"Rainbows are there!"
He exclaimed, as they passed.   "How exquisitely fair!
With what delicate touch is each soft color blended,
Till the eye fails to see where begun and where ended!
Here the artist, enraptured, may pause and admire,
And the wonderful scene will fresh genius inspire,
Till, perchance, the great theme might be mastered,—Art
       stand
By Nature's own side, proudly grasp Nature's hand."

THEON.

That art which most freely from great fountains drank
Must needs bend its head when 'tis placed in the rank
With Nature's least works.   E'en the light springing sod
Which we tread underfoot here proclaims Nature's God;
Appeals with a fervor, a freshness and beauty,
To man's purest thoughts and man's high sense of duty;
And teaches rich lessons where Art is yet still
In nearest approaches to Nature's great skill.

ETHRIC.

Pray tell me, what lessons?   You follow in gleaning,
Translating their speech, can you trace its full meaning
That tells of man's duty?   Let me learn here of you
To read the great volume unrolled to our view.

THEON.

I teach not their words; I would learn.   Yet methinks
That e'en as the tiniest atom that sinks
'Neath our feet as we walk, having one certain place,
If crushed from existence would leave some bare space,
Even small though it be, and unnoticed by all
Saving those in close contact;—if the pebbles that fall
In yon flowing water, their wide circles make;—
Then the least of mankind (how much greater!) must
            take
Some first prepared place.   Though the space be not wide,
All influence is felt: good or bad may betide
Another for some trifling word or light thought,
Which with blessing or ill for all time may be fraught.

" True," he answered, half musing, " yet may there not be
A class to themselves who may hear, act, and see
For self and self only? · As it were, this world's drones,
Undisturbed by the sound of the busy bee's tones;
Who, 'tis true, work no good, yet complacently civil,
At least do no harm,—spread no terrible evil."

" Nature knows of no idlers; her work must go on,
And all things that are must assist," said Theon.
" Some workers are active,—the wild, rushing breeze,
The stream that flows·peacefully on to the seas;

And others are passive,—but, acted upon,
Most certainly give their full share to work done,
And produce new effects.   So it is with mankind.
Those who work may press on ; those who linger behind,
Being used by their fellows, must give the rebound
Of this action to others.   In time 'twill be found
The task of their choice Nature yields as their own ;
Though seemingly tranquil, their power is known."

IX.

Ethric started ; the case was his own, and she drew
The picture so plainly his likeness he knew.
For an instant he turned, with a feeling of pride,
To make his defence, and then paused, for the tide
Of potent conviction rushed o'er him, and told
What Theon, unsuspecting, there bade him behold.
And he thrust back the past with a feeling of shame,
And a secret resolve, hence to win a new name,
Full worthy the friendship whose now valued beam
Might prove his awakening from some fatal dream.

X.

She caught the expression she scarce could explain,
And fearing, yet not knowing how, she gave pain,
Quickly spoke :
                  " For my years it becomes not to preach.
Life's beginners must first learn of life ere they teach.
I have lived much with Nature, and loved day by day
To give to my fancy what she would convey.
A maiden's light dreamings may scarce prove of worth
When boldly brought forward."

ETHRIC.

Not so ! They gave birth
To new purpose in me. You have proven a friend
I may trust to my life. Though the time we may spend
With each other be short, the light pebble you've thrown
Has rippled the waters. If years may atone
For long years misspent, then my manhood shall give
This holiest proof : I would learn how to live.
One thing I would ask. For the sake of the years
When as children we played, ere life's shadow or fears
Its pathway had darkened, let me have here some token
Of this happy meeting ;—some pledge that, unbroken,
Shall rivet my purpose, and which I may bring
When life has grown real. Some light, trivial thing,
Which memory will value.

XI.

A plain velvet band,
With the gold pin that clasped it, she placed in his hand,
And answered :
"Take this. When its echoes shall call
And its charm shall prove true, then at Rutherford Hall
A friend's kindest welcome you'll freely receive.
Your purpose is strong ; remain steadfast, believe,
And you shall be victor."

XII.

Did the sun's brightest beam
So suddenly fall that its blessing might stream
On the seed that was sown by the way-border there,
And cause it to bloom, and full, ripe fruit to bear?

CANTO FOURTH.

I.

THE summer had waned, and the autumn's chill breath
Robed the leaves in the beauty that heralds their death.
The birds took their flight to a kindlier clime,
And the year was full-crowned, and must soon yield its prime
To the snows of the winter, like white frosts of age,
And its record be turned to the past,—a sealed page.

II.

When the party returned from Niagara, Theon
Had remained at her home. Craving change whereupon
Her excitement to feed, Maud had roamed here and there
With her uncle, just pausing a brief time to share
The pleasure of novelty. Rest would bring thought;
And leisure with burdens of memory was fraught.
Grown weary at last, e'en of change, they had come
To Rutherford Hall. In that old-fashioned home,
Won by its welcome, its bliss, and repose,
She lingered at rest. Yet the craving which knows
Only change found her there. Came the day when the fate
Of the nation, light poised over partisan hate,
By the vote of its sons should be known. Through the land
Rolled low muffled thunders; from each rallied band
Sped men to their places. Her uncle must hie
To his far Southern home. Thither Maud, too, would fly.

36

III.

Guests had assembled in answer to call,
That old cordial welcomes of Rutherford Hall
Might echo again, ere the farewells be spoken
And the circle there gathered at last should be broken.
Through the rooms, here and there, passed Theon, still
    attending
Her guests' slightest wishes; her happy smile sending
To each a full greeting. At length, somewhat weary,
She sought 'mid her flowers a rest. Came the dreary,
Yet half-confessed thought, that in memory was one
Whom she missed in the throng,—missing him, was
    alone.
For Ethric had visited often and told
Of a new purpose found, of the dull self of old
Far buried away; and she blushed as she thought
Of the quick thrill of pleasure his letters had brought.
She shrank yet the more from Maud's cognizant power,
And pitied the life where the woman's full dower
To ambition once given, brought back in return
Ambition's sad harvest of ashes to urn.

IV.

Enjoying the stillness that marked her retreat,
Forgetting all else, she had dropped in a seat,
When the door gently ope'd :—

             "Think you thus to clude
Your guests? Pray allow at least one to intrude,
And remind you that many await her return,
Whose absence has taught them her full worth to
    learn."

4

V.

Harold Morton,—full thirty; majestic in mien;
With bearing of one who throughout life had been
Accustomed to govern;—who brooked no control,
Nor yielded to time, place, or creature. Life's whole
Had been a success. Not success that is won
By virtue of courage, or duty well done;
Which strengthens true manhood by calling out force
That had else lain concealed; but success in whose course
No foe had been conquered. With every assistance
By nature and fortune bestowed; where resistance,
From the first scarcely known, grew at length by its rarity
A thing quite unthought of. Success to which charity
Alone gives the name; and if truth should be spoken,
'Twere better to write the word " Failure," in token
Of lost opportunities. One could but feel,
With what e'er opposed him in life, he would deal
Not so much from conviction, the right to maintain,
As the longing possessed a full mastery to gain.
He strove for life's prizes, not seeking their blessing,—
But alone for this reason; he willed the possessing
Were it but to destroy them. Gifted with grace,
Cultivated and travelled, by birth claiming place
With long-honored names, had his life-current fair
Revealed but slight glimpses of deep whirlpools there.
To himself, though concealed, yet he felt their wild force;
Unsatisfied cravings marked unrevealed source.

VI.

Theon had instinctively shrunk from his kindness;
His lavish attentions, impelled by the blindness
Of wilful caprice; for her woman's ken told
'Neath the polished exterior, a heart uncontrolled,

Whose fierce passions held the full reins of his life,
And drove him at will here and there in its strife.

VII.

THEON.

My fault I acknowledge; all guilty I plead.
Of a hostess each moment some guest may have need.
Let us quickly return, that the wrong I have done
At once be repaired.

HAROLD.

   Of your guests there are none
Need you more than myself. May I not, then, detain
You at least for a moment? Be good and remain
Where you are. You are fond of your flowers?

THEON.

Yes, truly; for many and sweet are the hours
Since childhood, when they in their beauty alone
Have been my companions. Each plant is my own:
As I nurse and attend them, methinks I can tell
E'en their language to me.

HAROLD.

   And they know you as well?

Theon smiled as she answered:
   " I dare say they learn.
And now pray excuse me:—permit my return."

Harold stood near the doorway.

VIII.

HAROLD.

                 Your pardon ; but stay
One moment and hear what I must and will say.
Miss Rutherford, know you the passion that breaks
All bonds of control, and supremacy takes
In the heart of the man ?   Can fathom its power?
And portion the wealth it demands for its dower?
Nay, more,—dare you think of the terrible blight
Denial must bring it ?—the heart's deepest night.

IX.

She looked up in wonder.   His flashing black eyes
Fastened firm on her face sought her soul's full replies:
And his deep voice continued:

HAROLD.

                 That passion is love :
Triumphant o'er all, it arises to prove
Its legitimate place.   By the right of its name
I pleadingly come all its dower to claim.
Nay, turn not aside ; in my heart's sorest need
For the word that is life,—for your love here I plead.

X.

The haughty reserve of his manner was changed ;
The dark, secret face that had made him estranged
From aught that was tender, revealed hidden fire.
The madness of love seemed his soul to inspire.

Theon answered slowly :

                 " There are dreams that are dear
That oft rise before us: so vivid and clear

The outlines are drawn, we are apt to conclude
The vision is real.   The hand may seem rude
That sweeps it away; and yet is it not kind
To prove but a dream what no substance may find?

XI.

HAROLD.

You answer in riddles.   Your meaning explain.

THEON.

I would I could do so without giving pain.
You have dreamed of a love all enduring and vast,—
And the vision is fair.   But when years shall have passed,—
Ay, and they may be few,—you will wake to behold
The bright dream has vanished, its bliss has been told.
For the love of your heart seeks its self-enthroned shrine.

HAROLD.

Trifle you thus with a love such as mine?
There are those whose endurance may live sorrow down;
There are hearts that may love, and in time's waters drown
All trace of that love, and rise strong and secure,
Scarred, it may be, yet with strength to endure
And new power to love.   But I feel, I have known
That my turbulent nature hath one love alone,
By which, if 'tis gained, may its tempests be hushed;
If lost, every hope will be hopelessly crushed.
Lady, I plead.   There's a charm o'er my life
That has won me all things; let it give me my wife.
Pause ere you answer; I pray you beware!
On your word hangs the fate of my life turning there.

THEON.

And think you 'twere kindness suspense to prolong?
Think you love comes at will, like the air of a song?

4*

Believe me, the time will yet come that shall prove
The self, now exalting, controlling your love.
Let me pass, I entreat you.   To linger is pain ;
A once broken dream is not gathered again.

HAROLD.

And this is your answer !   Had the one great desire
Of my life here been granted, it had served to inspire
A firm, noble purpose to prove the full worth
Of pledges here made.   Now beware ! lest the dearth
Your refusal has left should encompass your path ;
Beware, lest your love meet retributive wrath !
For the storm may roll back in its force on your head,
And the lightnings avenge me, the love that lies dead.

XII.

He had gone ; yet his words seemed to re-echo still
In monotonous tone.   Seemed his dominant will
O'er her life holding sway.   A glad voice broke
Her revery at last.   'Twas her cousin who spoke.

XIII.

MAUD.

Theon !   Are you dreaming?   Nowhere could I find you.
Your guests are departing ; must one needs remind you
To bid them adieu?   Has some grim spectre made
A visit to-night?   Twine this bud in your braid :
It lessens your pallor.   Harold Morton has seen
The same ghost I think.   (Put the tuberose between
The sprays of geranium,—so.)   He has gone.
From the manner he galloped his horse down the lawn
One would think Tam O'Shanter ne'er equalled his haste.
There ! now you look better !   No time is to waste.

XIV.

MAUD'S JOURNAL.

" At last all are gone, and the household asleep,
Leaves the lone silent hours to me while I keep
My counsel with mem'ry.   The fortnight is past
Of my stay with Theon ; and yet e'en to the last
He has not come.   Fate has spared us the pain
Of one single meeting.   Henceforth it is plain
He has chosen his way.   Be it thus : evermore
Let our pathways diverge.   In the deep sacred store
Of the past let the secret be buried.   To-night
I o'erheard Harold Morton ; his words gave the blight
That my own heart has known.   Ay, in time be it said,—
' Let the lightnings avenge me, the love that lies dead.' "

XV.

The morning had come, had been said each " good-by,"
And the guests left the Hall on their journey to hie.
Theon was oppressed by the memory of all
That had passed the night previous.   She could but recall
Harold's feverish excitement, which seemed ill to prove
The depth and the fervor he pledged in his love.

XVI.

It was one of those picturesque, beautiful days
Of autumn, when Nature chants last hymns of praise.
Theon left the house for the free, open air ;—
Turned her steps to a nook, 'neath the old elm-trees, where
As a child she had loved every grief to forget,
And banish the cares which in childhood may fret.
Long she sat there, wrapped in revery, unheeding
The moments to hours in steady flight speeding,

Till a footstep had startled her.   Turning around,
She listened a moment, and marked the low sound
Of a man's heavy tread.   Springing quick to her feet,
With a bright flush of welcome she hastened to greet
Ethric Montgomery.

THEON.

           I have half-mind to scold you
Instead of to welcome.   Remember, I told you
Maud left us to-day.   What fates intervene
Preventing your meeting?

ETHRIC.

           Your kindness shall screen
My offence from your eyes.   There were cares to detain
Till the moment had passed, and all efforts were vain.
My regrets to your cousin.   So many, perchance,
Their tributes have paid where her graces entrance,
One would not be missed.

THEON.

           In that you are wrong;
For the family ties have been hallowed so long.
The son of her father's best friend, she should find
A welcome from you eager, cordial, and kind.

ETHRIC.

Did your cousin expect me?

THEON.

           Had she not the right?
Though pride held reserve.   Do you think it was quite
The courteous treatment that you should extend?
Mamma made excuses your name to defend.

ETHRIC.

My thanks to your mother. While she deigns to plead
In my poor behalf, I have no farther need
To utter a word.

THEON.

Thus exchanging regrets,
Your hostess, unmindful of all else, forgets
You are weary with travel. The morning was fair,
And tempted me out in the cool, bracing air.
Let us go to the house.

XVII.

ETHRIC.

Stay! Allow me to choose.
In token of peace, you will sure not refuse.
Let us sit where the elm-trees their full shadows cast.
Dear haunt of our childhood! How hallowed the past
Ever grows as we wander through life's tangled maze!
How cherished each scene of the long-ago days!
It is years since I left yonder village to roam ;
But my heart often turns to the quaint-shaded home.
It may be a fancy:—I've thought that yon spire,
On the old-fashioned church, pointed straighter and higher
Toward heaven; and the long-metred hymns and the
          prayers
Had more power to soothe and to banish our cares
Than aught I've heard since.

THEON.

That may be. But the present
Has surely its charms; for the past, howe'er pleasant,
Is dead to us now, save the lessons we've conned,
And the strength for new conflicts in future we've donned.

XVIII.

Ethric threw himself down on the grass at her side,
And looked at her earnestly while he replied.

ETHRIC.

That is true; yet methinks it were better the child
Could live longer the innocent days.   In the wild,
Restless course of one's life much is gathered of pain,
Much is lost of the purity never again
To be here recovered.   Could children but know
The breakers ahead, and the dark clouds that throw
A shade o'er their paths, think you not they would choose
The pure life of childhood, and glory refuse?

THEON.

Remember, in shunning the struggles of life,
That one also forfeits the strength which from strife
Is e'er to be gained.   Every rough battle won
Bequeaths new resources for work to be done.
Every wound that is suffered, 'tis true leaves a scar;
But hardier he that has gone through the war
Than he who ne'er witnessed a battle.

XIX.

ETHRIC.

                       Too true!
But hopes that are cherished must courage renew.
A friend you have proven in words fitly spoken.
There is more I would ask.   I have brought back the token;
Its mission is done; and I come in its name
To tell you of struggles a past to reclaim.
You found me the child shunning work I must do;
You aroused me to manhood, and held to my view

Man's holiest purpose, awakening the glow
Of long fettered strength. But you yet may bestow
A love that shall be the bright star of my life,
My one all in all! Speak, Theon! Be my wife.

XX.

Silent she sat, while her sweet face was bowed
And her thoughts travelled fast. Though the love that he
    vowed
Thrilled her innermost soul, she could utter no word.
One moment of silence, then softly she heard
Her name called, and Ethric's voice trembled.

ETHRIC.

                  Theon,

If the hope I have cherished has nothing whereon
To build its foundation; if down in your heart
No response is awakened; if henceforth apart
Our life-paths must wander, God knows that the light
Of my life will be shrouded in long, darkest night.
Yet still from afar, will the love I have brought
Shed its blessing on you, all unseen and unsought.
It would guard you from ill, from afar spread its screen
All sorrow and danger your pathway between.
Though silent, you do not forbid me to love,
And shall not in time love its worthiness prove?

XXI.

She lifted her face, turned it full to his own,
Endeavoring to speak. Ere the words could atone
For pain that her silence had caused, Ethric knew
That her heart answered his, unreserved and true.

XXII.

In the quiet of eve, by an invalid's chair,
A maiden was kneeling, and light on her hair
Fell a pale, wasted hand.   Hark ! the low words : " Dear
    mother,
Last evening I crushed from the life of another
A strong, avowed love, and to-day I have given
The love of my life.   Let the blessing of heaven
And yours, sweet mother, come showering down
My heart's sacred duty, my heart's love to crown."
And the angels bent low and the echoes were still
While the blessing was given Theon's joy to fill.

CANTO FIFTH.

I.

'Twas the evening that ushered the coming New Year,
Which loomed in the future all dismal and drear
With a people's forebodings.   The dark angry cloud
On the far-off horizon had grown till it bowed
With its weight over all.   Through the breadth and the
    length
Of the land, men were grouping, and counting their strength ;
And women were trembling and shrinking with dread,
While the lowering tempest that gathered o'erhead
Blighted their pleasures and hopes with its breath,
And spread o'er the land like the shadow of death.

II.

Already one State had withdrawn her fair name
From the circle of those for whom one common fame
So long had been cherished.   And others might make
The same irretrievable step which would stake
The fortune and honor of each loyal son
That rights be maintained and their freedom be won.
Would Virginia thus go ?   To Theon, Ethric's oath
Was recalled, and it seemed a strong hand which drew both
On to some dreaded doom.

III.
    For a full week or more
Ethric's letters had failed, and Theon puzzled o'er

Every possible cause.　Yet her womanly heart
Held sacred her trust, for her love formed a part
Of her life, and hence, guarding its sacredness well,
Its joy or its sorrow to none could she tell.
This eve, in the parlor, in twilight's soft gloom,
As sadly she pondered, Maud entered the room.

IV.

MAUD.

All alone in the shadows?　Come! ring for a light,
And cheerful in memory be this my last night
In the home of my father.　How oft as a child
I have longed to behold it, whose peace undefiled
His pathway has crowned!　Oftentimes have I hung
On his words with enchantment, as in his own tongue
He has told of sweet memories clustering here,
All hallowed in age, as in youth scenes were dear.
And here I have been!　Through the old homestead door
A guest I have entered.　A little while more
I shall bid it "Farewell!"　When your guest shall have
　　　gone,
Will a tender thought live of her visit, Theon?

THEON.

Broad is the roof-tree of Rutherford Hall;
Over far-scattered children its blessing will fall.
In each generation, who claims a place here
Shall in memory be cherished, find welcome most dear.
And when you shall leave us, though farewells be spoken,
The tie here rebound shall be steadfast, unbroken.

MAUD.

There are moments, Theon, when your deep, searching look
Fastened firm on my face seems to read as a book

My soul's inmost thoughts. At such times I have known
That you judged me as cold and as heartless as stone.
Believe me, time was, ere the stern icy breath
Of winter had frozen my young heart to death,
When I would have shrunk e'en as you from the world.
That has passed: here and there, on its swift eddies
    whirled,
I have lived but to see that love fades from our view,
And I laugh with the throng.

THEON.

            Maud, this cannot be true.
What were life worth were our lives here but proving
False above all things the great gift of loving?
'Tis better to trust and rejoice than to doubt;
For trust from within begets honor without.

MAUD.

Life is beautiful yet: you have seen but the flower
That blooms in the sunlight; you've not felt the power
Of the blast that sweeps by, till the light, brittle stem
Snaps in twain, and is trod 'neath the feet of all men.
You have read of love tried :—have you seen it in life?
Better the stern test should come ere the wife
Bows her head in her sorrow, and finds she has cast
Her faith on a tide that is hurrying past.

THEON.

Love must endure! Even old Mother Earth
May change from her course ere emotions whose birth
Were worthy the angels, shall bring forth but woe.
'Tis their mission to heal bitter wounds here below.

MAUD.

Human hearts are a mockery. Those that seem crushed
In sorrow to-day will ere long, their griefs hushed,
Be the gayest of gay. Ah! I once thought as you,
But the years have unfolded strange scenes to my view;
And I laugh in my scorn at the work I have done,
And the deep wounds are healed and new homage is won.
But believe me, Theon, that this heart made of steel
Has enough woman left it, at times yet to feel
A longing intense for the old childish trust,
And it weeps bitter tears o'er the hopes gone to dust.
The one tender chord that is unbroken there
Your own hand has touched and your power has laid bare;
As you sweep it anon, it will tremble and wail,
And the good that is in me is roused; but I fail.
Comes again the wild discord that mocks each endeavor;
Comes again the chill blast with its power to sever
All beauty from life; and the low chord is hushed,
And the hope that it gave me my own hands have crushed.

V.

Theon could not answer; she seemed as one awed
And subdued into silence. Compassion for Maud
And a new nameless shrinking from her filled her heart.
Maud slowly went on.

VI.

MAUD.

As our paths drift apart,
Theon, let me feel that the one gentle power
That has crossed o'er my life may yet linger each hour.
Turn aside in your truth from the mockery and woe
Which you cannot feel, which, alas! I must know;

In time e'en forget me, let no lingering trace
Of my presence remain, e'er a joy to efface;
But pause ere you judge me, Theon, and beware;
There are depths of the heart one must fathom to share.

THEON.

Dull indeed were the world could no heart ever feel
In accord with another.   Life's woe, like its weal,
Must be shared, that each state may its blessing bestow;
And, cousin, believe me, the grief that you know
(For your heart has known sorrow) yet with me shall find
A sympathy tender and lasting and kind.
Could my weak hand have power, unknowing, to sweep
The one tender chord, let it, cognizant, keep
Its full, richest harmony heard till the strain
Awaken your heart to its spring-time again.
Then your sorrow, unknown, shall be buried at last,
Buried afar in its grave of the past;
Whence only, though sad, sweetest memories shall come
Like dear angel fingers to draw your heart home.
Time is swift passing.   This evening must be,
As you have suggested, from gloom ever free.
Some light duties call me.   Excuse me, I pray;
Here are beautiful books uncle brought me to-day,
Perchance they may aid the dull moments to fly
The while I desert you.   A pleasant good-by.

VII.

Leaving her cousin, she passed through the hall
And opened the library-door, whence a call
Reached her ear.   'Twas her uncle stood there.
" Ah, Theon !" he exclaimed, as he wheeled a low chair

In place by his side, "I can hear your light tread
If I am an old man. Come! My sunbeam must shed
Some brightness for me. You shall bring me some thought
That is born of your youth and with cheeriness fraught;
For the year closes sad, and the doubts of my age,
Though faltering not at the right, read a page
Through the opening year of confusion and strife.
Fain would I forget it.

THEON.

                    The new year brings life,
And life clings to hope. See you not, 'mid the cloud
Which seems to envelop all things as a shroud,
That radiant star? Through the blackness its beam
Is struggling to show, like some bright, fairy dream,
A beautiful picture of this our fair land,
The land of the South. See! her sons proudly stand
Untrammelled as freemen; her statesmen renowned
Are honored by nations; her daughters have crowned
Her cause with devotion; her rights are maintained,
Her rank is asserted, her escutcheon unstained.
Ay, uncle! we look to that glorious star;
And seeing but that, though the pathway be war,
Though it wearily lead us through long, dreary years,
Through toil and sacrifice, hardships and tears,
In firm, solid rank will our men therein go,
In unswerving fidelity women will show
Their faith in the cause we espouse.

VIII.

                    "Little girl,"
Clyde Rutherford said, stroking softly a curl,
"The hardship and trial will come, but the star
Must brighten or pale 'mid the fortunes of war.

I have loved the old flag, for my grandsire fell
Its birthright to buy ; and my father full well
Its honor defended when England again
Had sought to disgrace its bright folds with a stain.
Even I, in its cause, can exhibit a wound
Received years ago upon Mexican ground.
And now in old age, thus to rank as its foe
Gives me genuine pain.   Yet a soldier must know
That duty is stern, and that honor yields naught.
Should fulfilment of these in your own way be fraught
With hope-bereft tears, may your faith then as now
Lead you steadily on, though in sadness you bow."

IX.

THEON.

Enough of this, uncle, or else you may make
Me a sorrowful sunbeam without power to take
One shade from your mind.   I am puzzled to-night
By various things.   Can your age bring the light
My youthfulness needs?   What think you of Maud?

MR. RUTHERFORD.

A plain question, truly.   Of course I applaud
Her beauty, her manner—

THEON.

Nay, uncle, I mean
What doubt so enshrouds her?   With few years between
Her own age and mine, yet she seems strangely old;
And I feel that her heart has a tale to unfold.

MR. RUTHERFORD.

Her heart none have reached. I have known of true love,
Wholesome and manly, enabled to prove
Its own lasting value, from which she has turned
As from some worthless toy. From her father I learned
That Ethric Montgomery loves her sincere :
She answers him lightly.—What ails you, my dear ?

THEON.

Nothing ; the draught strikes me chill. I will close
The hall-door. Say you, uncle, Maud knows
Of Ethric's true love ?

MR. RUTHERFORD.

    Ah ! my child, does not live
That man who can love, and in no language give
His love an expression.

THEON.
   Is he faithful yet ?

MR. RUTHERFORD.

I doubt not. Such natures but seldom forget
The heart's deep emotions. Theon, are you ill ?
Your face is like marble, your fingers are chill.

THEON.

No, uncle ; 'tis nothing.

MR. RUTHERFORD.

    Not once since she came
To this land has she met him. She hears of his name
Unmoved and serene.

THEON.

And yet, uncle, 'tis strange,
If he loves her, he seeks her not, e'en to exchange
The greeting of friends.

MR. RUTHERFORD.

No, my dear; there is pride
Co-existent with love. O'er the gulf that is wide
And yawning between them,—a gulf that is deep,—
Which Maud has affixed, it forbids love to leap
Till chance bridge the chasm.

X.

With sternest control
Theon silent sat, while the words through her soul
Like keenest darts pierced ; for no other must sound
The anguish she felt. Although gaping each wound,
Their bleeding must be for her own sense alone.
Their very intensity guards them unknown.
The whispered misgivings his silence must bring
Arose like a legion new daggers to fling
'Gainst her trusting-like love. But, their power to break
Rang the echo of deep, earnest vows that would take
Neither doubt nor denial. While helpless she seemed,
Shut out from the future of which love had dreamed.
Came clearly the words, " Co-existent with love
There is pride ;" and her poor, stricken heart seemed to prove
Their veriest truth. Still her uncle went on.

XI.

MR. RUTHERFORD.

I fear Maud is sporting 'mid rocks whereupon

Brightest hopes will be wrecked ; for the sirens that call
Woo her on to great danger. The passing footfall
Of years with their burdens may retrospect bear,
And awaken with Maud deep remorse buried there.
Where is she, Theon? Bid her join us here.

XII.

Glad to escape, e'en pursued by some fear,
Theon left the room. Once alone in the hall,
The great oaken door seemed to shut her from all
That her hope had held dear. Stunned, bewildered, and
        awed,
Clinging yet to her faith, thinking vaguely of Maud,
A moment she stood there. When, hush, on her ear
Fell the tones of his voice, so hallowed and dear.
Unable to move, in each calm spoken word
Her heart the death-knell of its happiness heard.

XIII.

When Theon left the parlor, Maud turned to the fire
And stirred the red coals, till they seemed to inspire
The shadows with life. But a fortnight before
She returned from her wanderings, and ere yet once more
A day with Theon, marked as some special treasure
A letter received with a bright flush of pleasure,
And quickly concealed. Chancing next to convey
Her mail to Theon, she had glanced on the way
At the covers,—and quick, past the night at the Falls,
Past the years intervening, her memory recalls
A chapter long buried. She watched Theon's face,
Marked the letter which brought the bright glow in its
        place,

And the secret was told. From her heart to her brain
The blood madly rushed, and a wild frenzied pain
Seemed her being to rack.

XIV.

Quickly passing Theon,
She escaped to her chamber, and sinking low on
Her knees, long she wept,—not the pure tears of love,
But of love smothered o'er, having power yet to prove
The trace of itself; all distorted by fate,
All deformed through her passion, till keen, jealous hate
Came forth from its grave, and its full venom hurled
With a will that would hunt through the bounds of the
      world
For the object it sought. Madly drying each tear,
She arose to her feet; marked each sound as if fear
Asserted control; took a once handsome case
From her trunk, where 'twas kept in some care-concealed
      place.
On its broidered lining an old letter lay:
She opened it slowly, as if far away
Her thoughts had now wandered. The same manly hand
As Theon's, although written in some foreign land;
And it breathed a devotion rich, fervent, intense;
An avowal of love, and a prayer that suspense
No longer might hover a cloud o'er his life.
It placed at her feet, should she then be his wife,
A name that was honored, a true loyal heart
To beat for her only.

XV.

A little apart
In her trunk, as a mere heap of rubbish, were scattered
A dozen such letters; and bright hopes there shattered

Were as trifles to her, cast aside in the dust
To grow old in the years, to be moulded or rust,
With never a sigh to their memory; but this
Had lain in its cover a treasure. One kiss,
Warm and impassioned, she pressed on the page;
Then, suddenly seized with a transport of rage,
She tore it in fragments, as from her she cast
Every tender emotion that dwelt in the past.

XVI.

Ah! there's many a rose hath its thorn; e'en the fairest,
The one we love best, the most fragrant, the rarest,
Conceals 'neath its beauty some power to wound.
So, 'neath the bright blossom of love oft is found
The keen thorn of jealousy. The blossom once taken,
The thorn should be carefully stripped off, or, shaken
By unguarded hand, it may pierce till the pain
Thereby caused is so great, that the treasure, deemed vain,
Is tossed far aside in impetuous haste,
And the blossom crushed low in the dust goes to waste.

XVII.

Though Maud had but evidence slight whereupon
Suspicion to rest in regard to Theon,
She had quietly taken each morning the mail
As it came to the Hall, and had found without fail
The letter from Ethric; this she had concealed,
And time had the secret she wanted revealed.
None but herself marked the sigh quick repressed
As Theon scanned the letters; no other had guessed
From her eyes' silent language her heart's plaintive query.
Each day she had seen her pass on with that dreary,

Sad look in her face. Ofttimes sympathy pleaded,
And her stilled, better nature was roused, but unheeded.
The blow was for him; blind, persistent, she hardened
Her own perverse heart and her cruelty pardoned,
By teaching herself that ere long 'twould be over,
Theon having quietly yielded her lover.

XVIII.

So the days wore away, until Maud's mamma, dreading
The burst of the storm from the clouds that were spreading,
Had summoned her child. Still Theon's patient sorrow
Was borne day by day, and increased with each morrow,
While Maud watched in awe. Had her cousin but spoken,
Or doubted, or murmured. She felt that unbroken
Her sacred trust lived. Could it be she had known
Love greater than Maud's? Seemed the wrong to have
    grown
In spite of the plea that no line had been read,
No treasure laid bare; evermore with the dead
Should their secrets be buried. Yet past her recall,
Maud shrank back from what she had done, and it all
Seemed a dark, dreadful dream, whose brief madness would
    urge
Her soul deeper down the abyss, on whose verge
She long stood and trembled; and in her distress
Her feeling of hatred was smothered. Confess?
To her cousin?—she could not; to Ethric?—and then
Came a burning desire to meet him again.
For the heart of the woman had opened once more,
Revealing the tenderness deep in its store;
And it pled for one moment of bliss, only one,
Ere the duty that summoned her strength should be
    done.

This granted, she thought to have yielded the past,
Removing each doubt that her purpose had cast.
Never pausing to think of the danger that lay
In the course she would take,—choosing blindly the way,
A note was despatched, and her pathway seemed smooth
And lighter her burden.   'Twas easier to soothe
Reproaches that haunted, by pleading the morrow
Would bring her the power to heal Theon's sorrow.

XIX.

Yet to-night conscience roused, when Theon's truthful eyes
Had turned full upon her in unfeigned surprise.
And since she had left her the pleading look came,
And Theon's full reliance in love's sacred name.
She could bear it no longer, but sprang to her feet,
Urged on by new impulse, the full fact to meet,
And comfort her cousin.   A step in the hall!
A voice she well knew!   Reeling, blind, lest she fall
She grasped a large chair; and she felt the old pain
Of jealous defiance, as there once again
She stood face to face with the man that had taught
Her heart the one love with its bitterness fraught.
As he gracefully bowed, she had marked in his eye
A coldness that sought all the past to defy.
No light salutation her lips could command,
And her tenderness froze 'neath the touch of his hand.
All pleadings were silenced her wrong to confess;
Theon was forgotten; what to her his distress?
Repentance had vanished; her cold tortured heart
Stood aloof in its triumph, saw moments depart,
Till the one that was left her in which to rewrite
The good for the evil had gone in life's night.

CANTO SIXTH.

I.

WITH the touch of Theon's tender hand in his own,
And her words in his ear, moved anew to atone
For his past useless life, Ethric turned with a will
To the path he had opened, and strove there to fill
Every hour with a purpose. Already in air,
In grandest proportions, were built castles fair.
The man was ambitious alone for her sake ;
His manhood was roused this new struggle to make
That she, when she stood by his side as his wife,
Might read o'er the record he made of his life
With a true, honest pride. And he brought to the shrine
Of idolatrous love all the wealth of the mine
That so long lay concealed. Dreamed he not that that power
Which aroused him to life by its magical dower
Would lead him to purpose of yet greater worth,
Receiving from God-given principles birth ?
That the delicate hand which so passively lay
In his own should yet lead him safe through danger's way ?
Dreamed he not of all this. For the present his star
Shone serene through the darkness. Though naught came to mar
      to mar
Its light and its beauty, the source of that light
Was hidden by reason of that very night
Which revealed him his idol. Night precedes the morning;
And light but reflected bursts forth in the dawning.

Do we love the star less when we know the true source
Whence cometh its brightness? Nay,—tracing its course,
We thrive in the life-giving rays. Often so,
By passion or prejudice darkened, we know,
Should truth in its grandeur burst forth on us there,
The very intensity of its full glare
Had served but to blind us. Like some beacon-light,
Truth's radiance reflected may shine through the night,
Till, dawn chasing shadows of error away,
We learn to receive and to welcome the day.

II.

Be this as it may. Ethric bent to his task
With vigor redoubled; no aid could he ask,
That the battle his own, when at last 'twould be done,
He might honestly claim the full victory won.
Often came letters so pure in their truth,
So filled to o'erflowing with bright hopes of youth,
They proved sweet incentives to action when weary,
And seemed the bright sunbeams to days long and dreary.
But the time came at length when the loved letters stopped,
And the days one by one in their steady course dropped;
But, oh, how monotonous! E'en as the rain
That patters and ceaselessly beats on the pane,
Till one fairly longs for the quick lightning-flash,
And waits with delight for the thunder's loud crash.

III.

One day, burdened down with forebodings and gloom,
Ethric restlessly paced to and fro in his room.
His old doubts arising in strength of the past,
Were seeking their long, dreary shadows to cast

O'er the star he had worshipped.   He heard on the stair
A light, bounding step; his door opened, and there
Stood his friend Edward Hastings.

IV.

EDWARD.

Well, Ethric! act one
Of our national drama at last has begun.
What think you of matters?

ETHRIC.

I fear me, to-day
In the signs of the times there is discord whose sway
Shall be felt o'er the land.

EDWARD.

Aye, the valor and might
Of every true man may be tried.   Be the right
Our motto and shield, and hearts sturdy and brave
Will close band together our country to save.

ETHRIC.

My life and my honor Virginia shall claim,
Whene'er is endangered her loved, stately name.
There are dark days ahead; for a while I believed
The storm would pass over;—that trust was deceived.
It gathers fresh strength, and ere long its full roar
Through the land will be heard from each far shore to shore.

EDWARD.

Life is before us: our right arms are strong.
What though the conflict rage fiercely and long?

No holier cause could our service command,
No dearer incentive could prompt us to stand
Its fury to meet.   Even then should we fall,
'Tis sweet to give country life, valor, and all
That manhood may prize.   I, at least, shall leave none
Holding place more than friends.

ETHRIC.

             And I !   Ah !   There is one.
Unless—again dreaming—

EDWARD.

                 Another romance ?
Trust me now as of old.   Whence came the bright glance
You fear may soon vanish ?

ETHRIC.

                 Your memory recalls
My playmate of old whom we met at the Falls ?
The story is short e'en as hope's brilliant span.
I loved her with all the full strength of a man ;
But one thing was needed full bliss to bestow,
And that—— (then he paused.)

EDWARD.

             Ah ! the balance I know :
You proposed ?

ETHRIC.

         She accepted.

EDWARD.

                 You trod upon air,
Never dreaming that life could again bring a care.

ETHRIC.

Not so; but I turned with a will to my duties,
Seeing everywhere bright midst its conflicts life's beauties;
Receiving her letters, sweet pledges of love,
And tokens of constancy time might yet prove.

EDWARD.

Well?

ETHRIC.

The letters ceased coming——

EDWARD.

Go on.

ETHRIC.

With no reason

Or traceable cause. Once again for a season
I've lived in full trust——

EDWARD.

Ethric, stop, if you please!

Let the past die forever. Its putrid disease
Must never be summoned the present to mar;
The wound has healed over, disturb not its scar.
The love of the present its full right must claim
To your clear, manly judgment. My dear friend, for shame!
Such hastiness wrongs her.

ETHRIC.

I would I felt so!

I would forfeit this moment my all but to know
That Theon is still true. There occurred me this thought,
She is young, and I fear more reflection has brought
To this love a denial. Such silence bodes ill
Where hope is impatient.

EDWARD.

You've written?

ETHRIC.

Ay, still
As of old, every day :—letters pleading for some
Given reason for silence,—yet nothing has come.

EDWARD.

Why have you not sought from her own lips to know
Her full, spoken reason?

ETHRIC.

This noon I shall go
To Rutherford Hall. There has been till to-day
A succession of duties demanding my stay.

EDWARD.

Where is Maud?

ETHRIC.

In the West.

EDWARD.

Have you met her yet?

ETHRIC.

No.
She'll revisit the Hall, when of course I must show
The respect that is due to the cousin and guest
Of those so long honored.

EDWARD.

Theon knows the rest?

ETHRIC.

About Maud? I've not told her.

EDWARD.

You should, lest perchance
She hear from another your early romance,
And thereby misjudge you.

ETHRIC.

Yes? True. Here at last
Comes a letter for me from the Hall. May it cast
Every doubt far aside! . . . Listen, Ed; this is strange:—
"A note from mamma has just caused me to change
My plans, and return. Ere my visit is o'er,
The pleasure I crave of a meeting once more
With a friend of the past. Two days from the morrow
I await you in Charleston. Permit me to borrow
One day from your duties.
"MAUD RUTHERFORD."

EDWARD.

There!
The gauntlet is thrown! Lift it, Ethric, with care;
For the past it revives.

ETHRIC.

Let me see: this is dated
December the 30th. She leaves, as here stated,
On the morn of New-Year.

EDWARD.

Do you mean, then, to go
To Charleston and meet her?

ETHRIC.

                      My dear Edward, no!
I shall go, as I purposed, to Rutherford Hall:
Will reach there to-night,—answer this, and learn all
That my heart seeks to know.

EDWARD.

                   As good omens attend you
The sunniest wishes that e'er could befriend you.
You leave in an hour. You know, too, that I
Return on the morrow. God speed you! Good-by!

V.

Soon Ethric was plunged in the tumult and din
Of a journey by rail; and that eve, at the inn
Of the old quiet village near Rutherford Hall,
With dreary forebodings he dressed for his call;
For thoughts of Theon and of Maud through his brain
Flitted fast, weaving backward and forward a chain
Of memory and sorrow, of hope and of pride,
Of love, reaching farther than all else beside.

VI.

He wended his way down the old winding road,
His fancies still moodily nursing the load
Of doubt that he carried. How strangely perverse
One's nature becomes when one seeks to rehearse
Or feed on one's sorrow! And Ethric grew colder;
His old cherished ideas of woman were bolder;
The while his true love, smothered o'er, was yet burning,
And filled his whole soul with unutterable yearning

To meet with Theon.   He crossed it once more,
The threshold he loved, unannounced passed the door,
And stood in the presence of Maud.

VII.

A brief pause,
As if he would seek in her manner the cause
Of her summons to him ; but that instant he needed.
The next, he had bowed.   Her confusion unheeded,
Was quickly concealed.   She again was the cold,
Imperious, calm, heartless creature of old.

VIII.

ETHRIC.

Your note I received, and at least you must say
That I hastened, Miss Rutherford, all to obey,—
Nay, even more than its message commanded,—
And have greeted you here.

MAUD.

It has been, since I landed
On this your own soil, full five months or more.
Allowing me thus on American shore
To linger ungreeted,—is that friendly haste ?

ETHRIC.

Your pardon I crave.   But afar through the waste
Of years intervening, recall to your view
The cause of our parting.   Unsummoned by you,
I could not presume that my call would give pleasure.

MAUD.

There you are wrong, what is dark thus to treasure.

A mere passing fancy is too light a thing
A single remembrance in brief time to bring.

ETHRIC.

" A mere passing fancy ?" (The partly-closed door,
Unknown to them both, added one listener more,
Who had caught Ethric's words.)

       " Your pardon, I pray.
I beg to remind you that still, day by day,
You smiled on the love that you knew had had birth,
And taught me to think that you owned its full worth.
That love was sincere and to guile was unknown."
(Neither heard near the door-way a low stifled moan,
Nor a swift, passing step. Ethric's words, whereupon
Her fate seemed to hang, smote the heart of Theon.
Feeling only the impulse from all things to flee,
Only craving alone in her sorrow to be,
She hastened up-stairs.) " When that love was made plain,
Was the hope only raised to be mocked at as vain,
That ' a mere passing fancy' in moment of joy
With the heart's deep emotions might carelessly toy ?"

IX.

Like a flash came the truth, and Maud saw the weak pride
That had thoughtlessly cast a rich treasure aside.
Her effort to taunt him by charging his love
With lack of endurance had served but to prove
Her own overthrow. It were madness to feel
That her folly had chosen life's woe from its weal.

MAUD.

Each heart is a riddle ; anon one may read
The riddle aright. Shall one's memory plead

For each one read wrong? Although injured, perchance,
They have played but their part in life's passing romance;
And life is too short to be dulled by the query,
What havoc is done? Nay! forget and be merry.

X.

Could this be the woman who years since had won
His first manly love? Had the deed she had done
Left no single thought of regret or remorse?
Ah! little he guessed of the deep-hidden source
Whence her action had sprung! Little knew that the
    grave
Where her still heart had buried the love that she gave,
Was disturbed by the tempests of time, torn asunder,
And the ghost had refused the deep sod to lie under.
Marking her keenly, he slowly replied.

ETHRIC.

At the feasts of the ancients, when full the bright tide
Of pleasure was flowing,—when light seemed to shine
And dance on the surface of pure, sparkling wine,—
When care was far banished, and gladness and mirth
All thoughts wooed away from the troubles of earth,—
Lo! the drapery parted by magical breath,
And the revellers sat in the presence of Death!
Hath the maddening career that will ride over hearts
No moments like this, when some memory parts
The curtains close-drawn, and reveals to the sight
Some phantom long thrust in the shade of the night?

XI.

Dared he thus to torment her? Her vengeance and ire
Rose anew in their strength, seemed her soul to inspire;

Yet he must not see their fierce tumult, and still
Their wild force was held by her resolute will.

XII.

MAUD.

Think you, then, there is life given love that will last
When the seasons have thrust it far back in the past?
Think you those passions the heart will still cherish,
That like some bright blossoms have birth but to perish?
They are but the spell of the moment; 'twere madness
To seek to preserve e'en in memory their gladness.
Having lived, there's but proof that they ever were born,
In life's fiercer passions, or some latent scorn
That ignores as mere phantoms of vaporous air
The loves cast aside in the past,—buried there.

XIII.

Ethric's eye met her own; and there in it she read
The abhorrence, the pity, with which the last thread
Of her talk had been followed.   Her own eyes grew dim;
For anger she cared not, but pity from him
Was utterly maddening; to be loathed, set aside,
By the man she once loved, to the quick stung her pride!
She thought of the triumph achieved by her hate,
And mocked at his sorrow.   But ere 'twas too late,
Ere her own weakness served every thought to betray,
She must banish the subject whose terrible sway
Could no longer be borne.

XIV.

Hence to light, current news
She carelessly turned; sought fresh life to infuse

In the talk of the moment; her visits South, West;
The places she saw; how received as a guest
In the land of her father; the last novel read;
Her favorite opera: all skilful she led
The way of their chance conversation hence, hither,
And none would have guessed of the one point whither
She bade it go not. Yet in each moment grew
Her fixed resolution to hide from all view
The motive that prompted the note that she sent:
Be its course what it might, that each coming event
From her should receive no control.

XV.

Then at last
Ethric paused in their talk.

XVI.

ETHRIC.

See, the moments fly fast;
Unannounced, I have entered. Permit me to ring,
That a message, our hostess, your cousin may bring.

MAUD.

Allow me instead. You may know that I leave
Very soon in the morning. Theon shall receive
Your message from me. I will bid you adieu!

She extended her hand.

ETHRIC.

Take a friend's wish that you
In your theories find no more cause for regret
Than the pain it may give us some joy to forget.
But pardon me, too, if I give a friend's warning
That the phantom whose power your pleasure is scorning

May yet by the touch of some calm, icy finger
Bid you suddenly stop in remorse long to linger.

XVII.

She passed from the room,—from his life thus forever.
A moment he stood, in his feverish endeavor
The whole to explain ;—then a servant returned
And brought him this note :—

> "I have recently learned
> The cause of your silence.   The secret is told :
> The new love has waned for the love that is old.
> Henceforth you are free to return to the past ;
> And oh, that so doing your action might cast
> Each trace from my memory of words you have spoken,—
> Every vow I have trusted and cherished, now broken !
> I have read o'er the grave of a love that was mine
> Its full, solemn dirge.   Let the cypress there twine.
> Return to the past,—to its pledges ; thereon
> Trace a friend's kindest wishes : that friend is—THEON."

XVIII.

Dazed and bewildered, he read the note o'er,
Pondered each word as if deep in its store
Lay some hidden meaning.   "The old love,"—"the new,"
"His silence,"—"vows broken,"—"released" ? was it true?
His answer was written in haste :

> "Hear me now !
> I pledge you my honor that each sacred vow
> I have uttered to you is yet steadfast and pure,
> Endowed with devotion and strength to endure.
> There is mystery here.   Reconsider, I pray,
> The note you have written.   Unbidden, I stay
> And await your reply."

XIX.

To him each moment seemed
The length of an hour. The firelight gleamed
From the old-fashioned hearth, scuding weird shadows
    there,
Which flitted like phantoms in recesses where
Heavy curtains were drawn. Howled the fierce wintry
    blast,
And it echoed his burden of sorrow.

XX.

                            At last,
Came a tiny white note. Eager, trembling, he read :—
" This moment, I dare not recall what is said.
I will see you to-morrow. Then truth shall give right
Its full, honored victory. Trust me. Good-night."

XXI.

That was all : he must wait. Ah! the moments move slow
When the heart but one spot in the distance may know!

XXII.

The old Hall was still, and the pale moonbeams crept
Through the casement, revealing Theon as she slept.
Her face like an infant's was sweet in repose,
And her breathing came soft. Flushed her cheek like the
    rose
In the freshness of morning. The door opened wide,
And a figure white-robed gently passed, seemed to glide
Like a spectre of night, treading light upon air,
To the bedside and gaze on the form resting there.

As if in her dreams, yet disturbed by some fear,
Theon gently sighed, while the gathering tear
Trickled down 'neath the lash.   Then a low voice spoke,
And its sound like a moan on the night's stillness broke :
" I have utterly failed !   Oh, Theon ! canst forgive
The hate that must conquer, the wrong that must live ?
From their strength unsubdued, do their wild terrors roll
O'er your innocent suff'ring, back, back on my soul,
And I dare not confront them !   In peace may you slum-
     ber ;
All hidden to you are the woes without number
Which the love of your life to my poor heart has brought ;
The remorse and the anguish of one moment's thought ;
You have made conscience madden me, e'en while I nurse
For his sake a frozen love's vengeance and curse."

XXIII.

Theon moved in slumber, and quickly away
The pale guest had vanished.   With earliest day
There were voices heard, and the farewells were spoken,
And Maud left Theon with no sign or no token
Of aught she had done.   But the hushed echoes wake
Mid scenes of the future confessions to make.

CANTO SEVENTH.

I.

THERE'S an old song that calls the great lesson of life
" The sad, sad lesson of loving." 'Tis rife
With sunshine and shade each in turn to unfold;
" But the saddest of loving is love grown cold,"
And better it is than this darkest of phases,
" That one heart should rest 'neath the beautiful daisies,"
For the heart robbed of love has been robbed of its all.
Having answered this highest, no ignoble call
May arouse it to life. It beats wearily on,
Perchance, with some fitful emotion, soon gone;
Oft craving life's stimulants, thus tossed about,
Testing and turning from all things in doubt;
Remembering the sunshine, yet shrouded in gloom;—
Ah! better than this is the daisy-crowned tomb!

II.

Brightly and beautiful dawned the New Year;
But the night that had passed left a shadow so drear
O'er the life of Theon, that, its promises fair
By a breath swept aside, she could see but life's care.
Down the long halls she wandered, through each chamber,
    dreary,
While restless and anxious, yet listless and weary.
In the rooms, now unused, where the old buried years
Had each woven tales of their hopes and their fears;

Tracing there by her fancy, through sympathy's chain,
The echo that answered her heart's minor strain.

III.

A sudden thought came. In a lone, upper room,
Shunned for years on account of its time-laden gloom,
Was a portrait, close covered, and no searching hand
Had dared since her childhood to break the command
That banished it there. So it stayed, and each scene
And the changes of life time had brought in between
That face and the living, till, left with the past,
Forgotten, unheeded, with rubbish 'twas cast.
And the story or legend that over it hung
As yet had been spoken by no mortal tongue.
Sped Theon to the chamber. 'Neath cobwebs and dust,
In a far quiet corner the picture was thrust.
She opened the blind, and the sunlight streamed through
And fell on the canvas, disclosing to view
A beautiful face. 'Twas a soft, dimpled cheek,
The rosy lips parted, just ready to speak.
The fine auburn hair richly twined, while a curl,
Half escaped, loosely fell. Seemed the long lash to furl
Over eyes soft and tender. Theon, gazing there,
Imagined she read in the countenance fair,
Yet softened and shaded, ingenuous thought,
And a heart, save of hope and of truth, knowing naught,
Its counterpart, none that she ever had known.
What fate had condemned to a solitude lone
This beautiful image? Theon's eager mind
Went to work with her fingers some fresh clue to find.

IV.

As she pulled at the portrait, a light, clinking sound
Was given, and, hastily turning it round,
She spied an old ribbon, which still seemed to cling
To a parcel; she brought it all forth.   A plain ring
Of broad, massive gold to the ribbon was tied,
Bearing these words : " My love-pledge."   Could this be a
  bride ?
Had her lover proved false to this pure, golden token ?
Had vows been ignored and the sacred pledge broken ?
Yet who could have dared upon Rutherford name,
So carefully guarded, so jealous of fame,
To have hurled this dishonor and shed this great blight,
And buried this love in its terrible night ?

V.

She caught up the parcel, and hastened to tear
Its faded, gray cover, when suddenly, there
Her eye caught the seal, and she paused as she read :
" Let my secrets lie honored as graves of the dead."
A tear fell upon it ; she smoothed down the trace
Of the rent she began,—laid it back in its place,
As a relic too sacred for curious eyes,
And turned to the image with greater surprise.

VI.

While watching it sadly, at no distant day,
She resolved that, by right of unlimited sway
Which from childhood she held o'er the time-honored Hall,
This portrait should come from the lone garret wall,
And hang in the cosiest, sunniest place
She could find as most fitting so lovely a face.

But servants were calling in search of herself;
Quick grasping the parcel that fell from its shelf,
And slipping the ring on her finger, she turned
From the past till decrees of the present were learned.

VII.

Face to face with her lover. The meeting was grave ;
Each felt for a moment constraint that it gave.
Ethric read in her countenance traces of sorrow,
Yet her manner composed seemed refusing to borrow
Aught of one's pity. Her eyes' mute appeal
Met his own with an earnestness making him feel
Her full, conscious dignity. Seen in his hand
Were her notes of last evening.

VIII.

ETHRIC.

Held by your command,
I have bided my time. Have the vows I have pledged
So lightly been guarded, so loosely been hedged,
That aught may have power to rend them in twain ?
Think you justice is done ?

THEON.

It is true that the pain
Of doubting awakens a greater one yet,—
And that, to be doubted. For one is regret
That one trusted ; the other wounds honor,—trust's treas-
        ure.

ETHRIC.

Pray why undeserved do' I bear its full measure ?

THEON.

Undeserved?—Say you so? Stunned, bewildered, confused,
Pleading still for your truth, my allegiance refused,
While hearing last night of your earlier love,
Your pledges to doubt. Self-confessed, you did prove
My right thus to judge you.

ETHRIC.

                Permit me to know,
From whom did you hear what has injured me so?

THEON.

From my uncle.

ETHRIC.

           Self-witnessed? I beg, when and where?

THEON.

With Maud here, last evening. The fates in whose care
Pass the spun threads of lives, led me on through the hall,
Held me fixedly there,—bade me hear you recall
The love you gave Maud,—bade me hear you defend
Its unsullied honor. Your language did send
Fullest proof to my mind. Was there need for aught more?
That instant of time fixed the broad chasm o'er
Which my trust could not pass. Lay dishonored with me
Your unreclaimed vows. Are you wronged to be free?

ETHRIC.

Nay, judge me not yet. Heaven knows that to you
I offered a love unimpaired, full, and true.
You wrong me; and yet I admit your full claim
To trust was withheld. Hiding nothing in shame,

I erred in concealment.   Theon, in your heart
Were your pledges approved?

IX.

                              His tones made her start;
He spoke the words gravely.

X.

ETHRIC.

                              No moment of pain
Would I give you unneeded.   Love knows but the plain
Unadorned tongue of truth: even so, it is best
Every doubt should be heard, or in peace laid to rest
Whence it never may rise.   From your cousin a message
Requested my presence in Charleston.   Some presage,
Your long silence gave, bade me answer it here,
For the days as they passed but confirmed me this fear.
I ask of you now, did the thought of vows spoken
In judgment recalled,—did your confidence broken
Lead you to this silence?

THEON.

                              Your reason should tell
This full explanation.   A woman's heart well
Doth guard her life treasures.   A step such as this,
If thoughtlessly taken, bodes little of bliss.
In sober reflection I answered your love.
But e'en as the call does the full echo prove,
Woman answers to man.   With no summoning word
Shall the echo yet thrust itself forth and be heard?
Enough, that it lived till the knowledge had come
That the harmony waking it henceforth was dumb.

XI.

The last lingering doubt Ethric harbored was dead.
The truth of Theon fullest radiance shed
Like halos around her; for Ethric discerned,
'Neath her dignified patience, devotion that earned
His trust unreserved. E'en the echoing name
Of the doubt he had fostered now put him to shame.

XII.

His nature was eager the wrong to repair
By instant confession. That page he laid bare
That had shaded his life,—told her freely of Maud,
How he judged womankind, till Theon swept the chord
Of his numbed better nature ;—how life should atone
For the one cruel doubt that had sought to dethrone
His love's rightful queen; and Theon reigned secure
O'er a heart whose allegiance was sacred and pure.

XIII.

Ethric heard from her lips of the days that had passed
With no letters from him; how, perplexed and harassed,
She had waited in silence, preferring alone
To carry her burden than hear the light tone
Of Maud's thoughtless mockery. Language so fraught
With bitterness oft, had forbidden that aught
Of her secret be uttered at times when it gave
A joy so great it must sympathy crave.
How at last she had heard Mr. Rutherford tell
Of his love for her cousin; how like the death-knell
Of her own cherished hopes that were ruthlessly broken,
Seemed the calm, earnest words that to Maud he had spoken.
Thus all was explained.

8

XIV.

ETHRIC.

Even now, in this room,—
So fresh with its memories of yester-night's gloom,—
This morn bright with sunlight that welcomes the year,
With the shadows be banished each doubt and each fear;
In full, lasting trust be established my vow.
Theon, Heaven knows that I offer you now
A heart which has learned th' inexpressible worth
Of all that it craves,—of the love that has birth
In motives resplendent with truth.   Having sought
For your constancy proof, having harbored in thought
E'en a doubt of sincerity, shrinking in shame
I can offer you nothing but proof that will claim
Your full trust in me.   There is left but one way:
The letters I've written and mailed you each day
I must find and restore.   Heaven grant it may be
That they merely were lost!   At this moment I see
(Rememb'ring the distance o'er which they were carried,
And knowing ere this that no letter has tarried)
Greater reason to fear the same motive detained
One and all on the journey.   That motive explained,
If harmless, shall pass.

      Then Theon read his face
Half expecting her answer :—

        " If not ?"

ETHRIC.

         To efface
A meaning unjust must the culprit retract
His motive, and, yielding the letters intact,
Injured honor appease.

THEON.

Come the issue to end?

ETHRIC.

I shall then at all hazards my honor defend.

XV.

Her surmise was right; for an instant her touch
Fell soft on his arm.

THEON.

I had dreaded o'er much,
Even more than I tell, that this course you might take,
And your life and my own by this fatal mistake
Forever be darkened.   Believe me, I shrink
From this your decision, as if on the brink
Of a terrible precipice, ragged and steep,
You were closing your eyes for the last, fatal leap.

ETHRIC.

'Tis woman recoils at the danger; but man
Dishonor fears more.

XVI.

All the bright color ran
To the face of Theon.

THEON.

Ah! that terrible charge
Is dishonor to woman.   The world proves at large
That even grave dangers a woman may brave,
Yea, gladly, if physical courage may save
Aught she has deemed sacred.   Which, think you, is
greater,—
That courage controlled by man's passion (his hater)

Which faces unflinchingly bullets and steel,
Sets its foot upon fate, crushes life with its heel,
Or that which can suffer unmoved, and can dare
To brave the world's scorn, that unstained it may wear,
In sight of high heaven, a radiant crown,
Undimmed by man's selfish impulse,—his life's frown?

XVII.

He answered her nothing.

"You know that your name,"
She gently continued, "is dearer than fame,
Than riches, nay, dearer to me than all earth;
God knows that the rather than it should have dearth
Of full, manly honor, my all I would give
That henceforth untarnished and sacred it live.
That courage is false that is seeking to lead
Your soul into danger. The honor indeed
It proclaims is not there. E'en as heaven above
Is greater than earth, and its precepts of love
More powerful far than aught else to control,
So greater by far is this courage of soul
That fears naught of earth. In its might 'twill oppose,
Both seen and unseen, every army of foes
Which the world marshals hither. The danger to life
Is less than the danger to soul in the strife.

XVIII.

A brief moment's pause.

ETHRIC.

Could you honor me still
If I quietly sit and receive to the fill
A dastardly motive? No! Slander conveyed
Must give its denial, or ever be stayed.

THEON.

You are right. Be your life all untarnished your shield;
Its well-proven honor the weapon you wield.
What virtue to brighten that honor has blood ?
On your soul there is left a dark stain by its flood.
Your life all secure against slander's foul breath
Will accomplish far more than could possibly death.
For patience achieves its grand triumph at length,
Where force having spent the full burst of its strength,
Having no more to spend, will all powerless lie,
And the foe unsubdued may its weakness defy.
The darts that are hurled 'gainst the adamant wall
Of truth must all harmless and helplessly fall,
Low to lie there 'neath the shame and disgrace
They bear in themselves, which no time can efface.

XIX.

Looking full in his face, Theon's tender brown eyes
Met his own with such meaning, such earnest replies,
That the man's soul was moved, and his deep voice broke
With strongest emotion as slowly he spoke.

ETHRIC.

I will think it all over, and if you are right
Perchance you have saved me from life's blackest night.
Heaven grant me that courage that all things may dare !
But, alas ! in confusion I still falter there,
Yet seeing afar as some glimmering beam
The light you would throw. Through my life may that
　　　gleam
Shine over my pathway, a beacon to guide
Through intricate mazes unknown and untried.

XX.

He extended his hand in farewell, and a minute,
No word being uttered, her own rested in it;
Then, moved by the impulse of sudden emotion,
He tenderly raised it,—with earnest devotion,
A kiss pressed upon it,—was gone.   All alone,
Sank Theon on her knees, and the low, subdued tone
Of her heart's supplication ascended to heaven,
A pleading that fullest protection be given :
" Shield him not only from dangers of earth,
But far greater dangers within that have birth !"

CANTO EIGHTH.

YOUR letter bore tidings that end the suspense
Which was felt through the land. In our righteous de-
    fence
The old tie is broken that strengthened the past ;
The great gulf is widened, the grand die is cast ;
And the future must bring to Confederate name
The cypress or laurel, dishonor or fame.
The deep, angry chasms the lightnings flash o'er,
While heavy clouds darken, the loud thunder's roar
Rumbles on through the land from each far coast to coast,
Like the tread of the vanguard of some mighty host.
Long Virginia stood still, and the world seemed to wait
And hang on the moment deciding her fate.
She has bided her time in her own stately strength,
And listened, and watched, and the world roused at length,
When, spite of the tempest that threatens to break,
In spite of her homes and her lives there at stake,
She arises in fulness of grand, conscious power,
And links her fair name with its time-honored dower,
With the fate of the resolute sisterhood there,
To defeat or to triumph the new flag to bear.

I have heard her loud voice. With the answering
    cheer
Waking thrill of response comes a great burning fear ;

For echoed afar rings your deep, solemn oath,
And its tones of authority hasten us both
Where the storm's wrath is greatest, where lightnings must
     flash ;
And I shudder in dread of the forthcoming crash.
The voice of our land has appealed not alone
To her sons. While their blood must for great wrongs atone,
And her altars are waiting their lives to receive,
Her daughters are summoned. I feel, I believe
That with true Spartan zeal they will answer the call,
And, yielding their dear ones, their treasures, their all,
Be none the less brave though no weapon they wield,
Be none the less resolute never to yield.
Round the offerings they place on their loved country's
     shrine
Shall halos of purest refulgence entwine ;
For, sundering their heart-strings, still living they die,
And self is forgotten. The low, smothered cry
Of grief is unheard, as their own hands will bring
Rich offerings here ; gentle voices will sing
The war-song in triumph, the while echo there,
Heeded not by the throng, piercing wails of despair.
Your letter has told me the step you must take.
Heaven guide you therein ! May the clouds ere long break,
And, the storm having passed, may the future bestow
Its benison crowning the past tale of woe.
The love we have vowed shall the present inspire,
Receiving its baptism even through fire ;
And, faithful throughout, may it prove the full worth
Of the purest emotion bestowed upon earth.

There are times in our lives when the burden of thought
Apprehension may give makes us quick to see aught

That may be e'en remotely caught up in the chain
That is traced and retraced like a well-worn refrain.
A day or two since, came a letter from Maud,
Whose tenor has swept the inquisitive chord
Of my nature.   Permit me a portion to quote.
She is visiting England at present.

She wrote:

" Our hostess, an elegant lady, whose age
Crowns with beautiful halo the well-written page
Time has made of her life.   Rumor says in her youth
That her heart and her hand she had pledged in all
     truth
To a lover who dwelt in her own native land,
The land of your birth.   But that delicate hand
Was sought by another, whose family name
For long years had borne the well-earned badge of fame.
The maiden's heart yielded to visions of power;
Forgetting her lover, she fled at the hour
When he deemed her best, leaving home, friends, and all,
In obedience true to Ambition's first call.
But the husband grew cold, (what was that? she had
     wealth,)
And the dissolute life which he led, as by stealth,
Robbed the man of all virtues which claim the respect
A woman may give, until, forced to reject
Every hope of reform, she had nobly endured
And suffered through years that to suffering inured.
As his widow she lives : now a fair dame, possessed
Of personal grace, with this world's riches blessed.
That is rumor,—no more.   Never one single word
Does she mention referring to lover or lord.
'Tween the past and the present she draws a thick veil;
Yet methinks there are times when sad memories trail

Their shades o'er her face, and I wonder if yet
There lingers the trace of some cloud of regret.
One night, as we sat in the tapestried hall,
We were talking of love, of its influence, and all
Of the phases it takes, and I told her of you,—
Of your old-fashioned idea, esteeming love true;
Thinking, perchance, by some tact I could break
The long-imposed silence, and memories wake
That begged for expression. The manner she listened,
The tear-drop I saw on each eyelid that glistened,
Spite of efforts to hide them, I own, made me start.
Like you, she wrings from me a reverence for heart.
She heard me in silence, then quick left the room,
And quietly passed, like a ghost through the gloom,
Up the old winding stairs. There are times when I
    shrink
Back in horror from self, as I cannot but think
Of what might have been and what is. Does a stain
Like an unfading blur o'er my life thus remain?
I have thought of your words,—' It is better to trust;'—
Have I cherished a serpent, and forth from me thrust
The pure and the good and the power to do right,
And shrouded my young life in terrible night?
Think you evil of me? As you turn to the past
And read there my life with your own, does it cast
A weird, gloomy shadow? Theon, can there live
That light in your life which to mine light can give?
Do I talk strangely thus? Never mind! I will laugh!
Be my own self again,—throw my gloom e'en as chaff
To the light winds of pleasure. I'll drink to the fill
Of the cup that will bid every spectre be still
That may rise to condemn. I am gayest of gay.
What to me is the past? I know only to-day.

Why yet come the times when the mockery is awed,
Made dumb by the voices that still haunt me,—MAUD."

I have read and re-read, and have paused to recall
Many times when her lightness seemed forced. 'Neath it all
I know there is bitter remorse lurking there,
As a worm nestling low under flowerets fair.
Methinks of all things this the saddest to find.

Concerning her letter :—There is in each mind
Of quaint superstition some lingering trace,
Some fanciful thought that anon finds its place
In every-day life.   Who can be this fair dame
Whose long-hallowed memories were roused by my name?
What was the chord in her own life that brought
An answer to mine with such memories fraught?
Like the branches which, meeting, long stems intertwine,
Some link of her life must be woven with mine.
The portrait that hung in the lone garret gloom,
At my earnest request, is removed to the room
Where I oftentimes sit ; and the fair, lovely face
Brought out in the sunshine is clothed with new grace.
As yet I have heard its sad tale from no tongue ;
It rests in the mystery that o'er it has hung.
Two persons must know :—one, my uncle,—the other,
Who smiled at my whim and indulged it, my mother,
Yet quietly bade me refer not again
To a subject so laden with heaviest pain.
The parcel close-sealed I am certain could shed
Some light.   It is sacred ; perchance with the dead
Its secrets shall sleep on in silence forever ;
The veil that conceals them no stranger may sever.
The ring with your own shall remain on my finger,
And its motto and memories ever shall linger

Like some holy talisman potent in spell,
The love that is pledged guarding mutely and well.
I have fancied the face looking down on me now
Perceives, as in life, the new pledge of my vow,
And follows its presence with some holy blessing,
As if the past love were the young love caressing.
The fate of Virginia, your fate, and my own
Are inseparably linked.   Must the young love atone
For the waiting and pining and suffering and sorrow
The old love has known, ere it meet the bright morrow
Of peace and of happiness, welfare and rest,
With which the pledge kept, must as surely be blest?
The portrait, the package, Maud's hostess again,
In fancy have woven themselves in a chain
Which twines through my life, through my love, reaching on
In the future now threatening and dreary.—THEON.

CANTO NINTH.

I.

A STATELY old mansion was Rutherford Hall:
For time had dealt lightly there, while the footfall
Of years had passed by it, each weaving some tale
Of love, hope, or sorrow, which now, like the pale
Wan ghosts of the past, hovered over the place,
Here marking some chamber, there leaving some trace,
And pointing all for their subjects where waved
The willows in sadness. On each stone engraved
The name of some Rutherford proud. Sire and son
And son's child and grandchild, their life's labor done,
Slept peacefully there, while the breeze a dirge sang
Through the boughs of the willows; and young voices rang
Down the wide spreading lawn and through the elm grove,
While the guardian trees waved their old branches above.

II.

'Tis all quiet now; and the wind murmurs low,
And kisses the leaves waving softly and slow.
The long shadows creep from the vine-covered wall,
And bird warbles to bird his last, sweet, evening call.
On the broad, gravel way, with a dull, measured tread
Walks Theon to and fro; sadly drooped is her head,
And listless she seems to the beauty around,
Intent upon catching some yet distant sound.

Her light robes are changed for a deep mourning dress;
And a fresh-sodded grave tells the orphan's distress.
Sorrow's gaunt footstep is marked through the year
That has passed since we saw her. Anon a bright tear
Is seen on her eyelash, and trembles and glistens,
While, trained by long waiting, the quick ear now listens;
The stir of a leaflet, the flight of a bird,
The brook's gentle murmur,—no sound is unheard.

III.

A child, she had gathered the bright flowers that grew;
Time had revealed her the stinging thorns too.
Her father's one idol, his death the first grief
Of many that since had been merged in the brief,
Sad tale of her life; and each dark rattling clod
That fell on that coffin, had shown her her God
In His infinite strength both to make and destroy,
While she in her weakness must bend.

IV.

Years of joy
Had thrown that drear picture far back in the past,
As some softened background, on which till the last
Fond Memory lingers. The sweet dream of love
Had beamed on her pathway as light from above.
Pure, earnest, and trusting, the spirit of truth,
This first and her only love, beautified youth.
Instinctively scorning the wilful coquette,
Who wins but to trample some other heart yet,
And counts each one past, that has suffered and bled,
Each hope that is raised to be mocked at when dead,
As so much of victory,—tokens of worth,
(But, alas! withered laurels in years knowing dearth

Of the faithful devotion the heart longs to find,)
The depth of her own love had fostered a kind
Regard for another's.   The reverence she felt
For love in the abstract, had taught her that, dealt
With harshly, a sensitive plant it would die,
And broken and drooping its tender leaves lie.

V.

Thus, knowing no motive of conquest or power,
The love that she gave and had pledged 'neath the bower
Of her father's old elm-trees, was earnest and pure,
Could brave all things, bear all things, trust and endure.
In the strength of that love she reposed, and believed
That what she had given she freely received.

VI.

For Ethric had proved himself manly and strong;
A nature to whom love is not as a song,
That catches the fancy by some varied trill,
Which dying when echoed leaves all again still.
When love quickly comes, like the meteor's flash,
It often dies quickly; its short, brilliant dash
Scarce leaving behind it the pang of its sorrow;
Only the longing from all else to borrow
Excitement still greater.   The first quiet ray
That heralds the morning is feeble and gray;
But steadily grows, till the fierce, burning light
Of noonday bewilders and dazzles the sight.
And such love was Ethric's.   His purpose in life
Became to him earnest and dear, for his wife
Must learn to lean firmly upon that strong arm,
Which henceforth must tenderly shield her from harm.

They felt in their truth that a blessing from Heaven
On each sacred vow had been graciously given.

VII.

Through the land, far and wide, rang the bugle's loud call,
And men must be off to do battle and fall,
If need be, for home, and for rights, and for name
That was dearer by far than a warrior's fame.
Ethric was needed, and she must be still
And hush that wild cry of her heart by strong will.
How noble he was!   Filled Theon's heart with pride
As her hand touched a moment the sword at his side.
The steel glistened bright, but 'twas hard, and so cold;
She shuddered and dropped it.   How strangely grown old
She seemed in that instant!   Could weak woman bear
More anguish and live than was heaped on her there?
The moments were flying.   Ah! Memory's spell
Hovers over each one that had echoed " farewell."
Again she repressed the wild flood that would rush
Unrestrained to her eyes,—bade her murmurings hush.
She felt the strong clasp of his hand, and one kiss
As his soul had met hers, a brief moment of bliss;
Heard the " God bless you, darling!" and then,—he was
        gone;
And the long-pent-up flood had burst forth.   Slowly on
Time had wended his way through the one dreary year,
When cheered by his letters she struggled to bear
The burning impatience to welcome him home,
And learn to wait bravely till respite should come.

VIII.

This evening arise gloomy visions of strife,
And dark, misty phantoms, and weird phantoms, rife

With one fearful idea, and one sacred form,
Around which seems to centre the wrath of the storm.
Each object she passes is linked in the chain
That draws her own soul in that vortex of pain.
Right there, where she walks, were the words spoken
    low;
Right there, had she promised her love long ago:
And there she is waiting, while Ethric away
Braves danger and hardship. But, oh! thus to stay
In weary inaction and dreadful suspense,
Her loved one in peril, is torture intense.

IX.

That morning the wires had flashed o'er the land
The news of a battle: 'twas fearful and grand,
And "Victory ours!" brought to each Southern heart
A fervent "Thank God!" But the price! Who must
    part
With loved ones to meet it? And stern men bowed low,
While pale women trembled. God spare them the blow!
With others Theon had exultingly cried,
Then trembled in fear, while the swift-surging tide
Of wildest misgiving had flashed through her brain,
Each nerve stretched its utmost to bear the great strain.

X.

Ye heroes! who march with such resolute tread
Over graves of your comrades through blood you have
    shed;
Who stand in your places like some bedded rock
To be hewn by the sabre or ground by the shock
Of foe's fiercest cannon-balls; men who can wear
A smile in the battle, and undaunted dare

Take your lives in your hands, and defiantly stake
Your honor, your welfare, that fortune may make
You conquered or victor; whom conflicts inure,
Ye, men! Can ye know what it is to endure?
To patiently wait through the long lonely days?
To watch through the night, praying God send the rays
Of daylight to scatter the darkness whose gloom
Seems hanging o'er all things like some fatal doom?
To know that the one who of all upon earth
Is dearest,—whose absence would cause the great dearth
Were all others here,—to know that that one
May face death itself, ere the day shall be done?
Inactive to sit, and unmurmuring wait,
And bear a brave heart for each new-coming fate?
Ah! this takes a God-given courage, not human.
Ye, heroes of battle, give honor to woman!

XI.

Theon waited long; but at last her trained ear
Had caught the right sound, and a deep, crushing fear
Rooted her firm to the spot, while her face
So colorless grown showed each agony's trace.
She moved not, nor spoke, while a foamed, panting steed
Approached through the gate-way, exhausted from speed,
And her uncle dismounted. As swift glances met,
There was need for no question: the look of regret,
Of kindness and sympathy, tender yet grave,
The tidings long waited for, instantly gave.
Ere yet could the story be told, animation
Had yielded at last to her grief's usurpation,
And fainting she fell.

XII.

As a vague, breaking dream,
Was her senses' return : for the flickering gleam
Seemed only to show the intense darkness there,
In her life that awaited like some blank despair.
Her uncle had sought for words kind, and most tender,
As if from the blow his strong love would defend her,
To tell her that Ethric was missing, not dead,—
Only lost, since the battle. At the one feeble thread
Hope had left her she caught, and it seemed now to wield
A power that drew to the sad battle-field.
Perhaps he was wounded, was suffering ; her place
Was then at his side. At least might some trace
Of his fate be revealed. As she earnestly pleaded,
Her guardian felt that prompt action was needed
Her grief to control ; and he promised the morrow
Should bear them away. Love was facing its sorrow.

XIII.

In anguish she felt that her sun was gone down ;
Her pathway lay forward beneath the stern frown
Of fate ; she would tread it right bravely and take
Her place where most needed. For Ethric's own sake
She must live on and suffer. There is that in love
(A birthright decreed it, its birthplace to prove)
That makes the heart loving toil on in its woe,
Forbidding its breaking. Each agonized throe
A token becomes that the fierce stroke which wounds
Gives proof more abundant of love that abounds.

XIV.

Heroic in anguish, yet numbed by distress,
In realization of great loneliness,

Theon closer drew to the one loving heart
That was left her to bear of life's burden a part.
Clyde Rutherford, turning again from his age,
And meeting her years, paused to re-read the page
That time had long buried. Might she then recall
The warmth that was needed? The future a pall
Throws over each question. One has but to face
The duties enrolled there, and make one's own place.

CANTO TENTH.

I.

ONCE Israel's king, in a recreant hour,
Elated by fame and the grandeur of power,
Complacently scanned o'er his princely domain,
Recounted his conquests, the foes he had slain,
Exulting in might, bade his captains go forth
And traverse the land east and west, south and north,
And number the people,—his people who drew
Valiant sword in defence of his cause just and true.
What to him was the might of the numbers untold?
What the value of strength? what the worth of his gold?
For that marked, chosen people were marshalled and led
By One who waits not for a host's mighty tread;
And foes had been conquered and victories won
By Him who commands, and, lo! all things are done!
Jehovah in wrath on His servant looked down,
Made him feel the great wrong, made him groan 'neath
      His frown;
And the much-boasted power, the valor, and might,
Must suffer, that pride should not stand in God's sight.
Then the Lord bade the king lay his sceptre aside,
And know his true weakness, while he must abide
His choice of these three: Should Famine's gaunt face
Be seen through the land, leaving there ghastly trace?
Or War come with all the wild demons of woe
That tread in his footsteps and mock at each throe?

Or Pestilence shed over all that foul breath,
To change life and hope to despair and to death?
The monarch bowed low to the Almighty will;
The boaster was gone, but the man lingered still.
Humanity shrank from the passions of man;
Awed, humbled, it turned Divine mercy to scan;
And David besought that the hand of his God
Should wield the death-sword as his chastening rod.

II.

Man still is the same.   As we turn every page
That carries us over the tale of each age,
There we find wrote in blood, all the horror and dread
That humanity feels when the terrible tread
Of War shakes the land; for it wakens to birth
All the venom of demons, and frees it on earth.

III.

For more than a year had the battle-tide rolled
O'er a once happy land; and the death-knell was tolled
Over many a hope that was brilliant and fair,
But deep buried now, and low crushed by despair.
And men threw themselves in the vortex of fate,
Blindly yielding control to that fierce demon, Hate,
More fearful in nature, in power more unfurled,
Because against brothers and countrymen hurled.
Forgotten those days that were stored in the past,
When, shoulder to shoulder, and true to the last,
Their fathers had rallied one foe to repel,
Moved alike by one love, bound alike by one spell.
That time was long buried, and over its grave,
Over memories of those who had perished to save

The land of their birth, ran the dark, crimson flood,
Brother's life against life, brother's blood against blood.

IV.

The wild current poured its full force o'er the plains
Of stately Virginia, there leaving remains
Of once happy homesteads and once joyous hearts;—
In their place all the havoc of war's fearful darts.
Twice had been heard the dull tramp of a host,
Marching on to their homes with vainglorious boast ;
Twice had Virginia's sons rallied in might,
With sons of her sister States pressed to the fight;
Then, ruthlessly torn, the invader fell back,
But leaving the deep marks of woe in his track.
Yet again came the sound of his footsteps afar,
Yet again came his legions equipped for the war,
With forces redoubled, a will to destroy,
And, certain of conquest, exulting in joy.

V.

In defence, about Richmond, the city at stake,
Were Southrons encamped, and the foe must there break
Through this resolute line ere the goal be attained
And the prize so long sought for in triumph be gained.
Alas! ere that time for the blood that should flow !
Alas! for the agony strong hearts should know !
Alas! for humanity vaunting in pride,
Yet working the ills that itself should betide !
Defenders were gathered, and many a tent
Bore witness in silence of home-circles rent.
And in one, with brows knit, as if lost in deep thought,
His head bowed with care, e'en as one who had brought
Life's strength to life's battle, the General stood.

He seemed to be waiting; each sound in the wood
Made him start in expectance.

VI.

　　　　　　　　　Full many have won
High places in fame, for their valiant deeds done;
There are those who are honored for intellect rare;
And Genius has gained for her sons a place there:
But few are the crowns 'mid whose laurels entwine
Bright amaranths telling of virtues that shine
Resplendent and pure.　Hath the swift hand of Love
These undying garlands of rare honor wove;
And laurels from blossoms immortal shall gain
New power their freshness through years to retain.
Behold!　In the future, as long, brilliant pages,
Bearing record of statesmen, and warriors, and sages,
Be unrolled and re-read,—when the touch of the years,
And a nation's experience, learned through the fears
And the hopes of each new generation leave bare,
The motives that gained for each name a place there,—
The amaranth bloom with the laurel shall be
Entwined in the chaplet of—Robert E. Lee.

VII.

Re-write them, O History!　Sunshine and tears,
(An epitome grand of those terrible years),
The glory, the triumphs, the honors all vain
That marked the events of that summer campaign.
Chickahominy thundered McClellan's defeat,
And fierce were the conflicts that marked his retreat
To sheltering gunboats.　The course had seemed plain
That the foe would pursue, and a force to detain

For Richmond's defence, should McClellan attack,
Had been Lee's decision. Then quick, on the track
Of Pope's gathering army, must Jackson be hurled,
And the loved Southern flag o'er his path be unfurled.
Again the fierce cannons had poured forth their wrath,
The death-dealing stream crossed the enemy's path,
And famed Slaughter's Mountain to bright hopes had given
A full renewed promise. The foe that had striven
The homes of Virginia, her rights, to possess,
Lay stunned, and a pause seemed to mark his distress.
Then quick, plans were changed, and McClellan recalled,
That by force full united the Southrons appalled
Be soon overwhelmed; and afar, came the tread
Of three armies converging, their furies to shed
In one mighty storm that should scatter and break
The lines that might rally this struggle to make.

VIII.

What wonder that, pausing on that summer's eve,
And marking the records the past year must leave,
That Lee should have turned e'en from victory in sorrow,
Well knowing the woe and the want and the horror
With which had been shrouded his loved, native soil!
Ah! ye, who hear only of war and its toil
By messages brought over safe stretching miles,
Laden full with excitement which suffering beguiles,—
Who sit in your homes screened from bullets and fire,
And read of the struggles that fierce thirsts inspire
For yet greater glory,—can ye, sheltered, feel
What it is when the bullets and cold clashing steel
Are heard at your doors?—when your homes are laid
     waste,
And your wives and your little ones made there to taste

The gall of war's bitterness? Know ye the stream
Of blood that may run where your hearth-fires gleam?
Can ye feel with the people that bravely lay bare
Every long-cherished idol, each hope grounded there,
In stern resolution their rights to uphold,
Nor shrink from the agony strife may unfold?
Can ye wonder their leader should pause as he scans
The terrors to follow his well-matured plans?

IX.

A quick step was heard as he pondered the while;
The General looked up with a welcoming smile
As Ethric approached him and gave the salute.
He was clad for a journey, the spur on his boot
Clinking light with his footstep; his countenance, strong,
Told a purpose fixed, steady.

X.

                His General gazed long,
As if reading him well.
                " I have sent for you here,
Montgomery," said he, " having watched your career,
And marked you the soldier that now I most need:
This mission demands trust, and caution, and speed.
Jackson is now, with his veteran force,
Harassing the foe near the Rapidan's course.
These orders bear thither. God speed you in duty!"

XI.

Ethric sped on his journey. Calm night, in its beauty,
Fell slow o'er the scene, while each bright, twinkling star
Promised light, promised hope, as some haven afar.

With spurs to his horse he rode rapidly on ;
No sound broke the stillness, save now and anon
The low p'aintive cry of some wild woodland bird,
Or flutter of leaflets by light breezes stirred.
With every force bent to succeed on his mission,
And a deep, earnest prayer for the speedy fruition
Of each Southern hope, Ethric pledged his whole strength
Of heart and of purpose, that time should at length
Fully prove himself worthy the trust he had won,
And crown his name yet with more valiant deeds done
In behalf of the land of his love and his birth,
Now seeking a place 'mid the free names of earth.

XII.

On, on through the darkness, the sound of each hoof
Ringing loud on the ground. How the warp and the woof
Of our lives here are blended, through each changing hour,
While the shuttle is held by Invisible Power,
And no thread is broken, and tangled no skein,
Only waiting the future where all shall be plain !
God speed thee, brave warrior, and bring thee at last
Safely on to the goal, with all mystery past !

CANTO ELEVENTH.

I.

'Twas the eve of a battle. The old hallowed ground
Of Virginia had ere this marked many a sound
Of fierce, raging strife. In the years long since dead
Her sons' bravest blood had there freely been shed;
And proudly, she counted full many a name
Well honored and wreathed with bright circlets of fame.
More recently still had field, woodland, and rock
Re-echoed the roar of the cannon's wild shock.
Yet it was not enough. Soon again in her blood
Would the land be baptized; soon again would the flood
Pour its dark, crimson torrent, and fearfully roll
Through many a home, over many a soul.

II.

O'er the far-renowned ground, on the battle-swept plains
Of Manassas, whose greensward was dyed with the stains
Of patriots' blood but a short year before,
Stretched the long line of battle, and solemnly o'er
The sleeping battalions night's canopy spread,
Each star twinkling bright, like a sentry o'erhead.

III.

There's a hush o'er the scene, there's a stillness felt there
That startles and awes one. To-morrow will bear
Full many a soul that now sweetly reposes
To that mystical sphere which all mystery discloses.

112

Unmindful they sleep,—weary men who have known
What it is to brave hardships and stifle each groan.
Perchance the bright spirit that governs our dreams
Has touched with her sceptre those eyelids, and beams
In pitying love on each battle-doomed one,
And pictures bright visions of noble deeds done.
There rests the aged father, and close by his side
His boy, in the promise of manhood's full pride.
On the field of the morrow will gray locks and brown
Face the foeman together. Shall either lie down
'Mid the smoke of the battle? Will life's final page
Tell the bright hopes of youth or the sorrows of age?

IV.

Farther on, sweetly sleeping, forgotten all care,
Lies one strong in manhood. The dream-spirit there
Is working its mission. Anon a sweet smile
Steals softly o'er sun-burnished features, the while
The large gathering tear-drops fall over each cheek;
For true men may weep and yet never grow weak.
Perchance 'tis a husband and father; perchance
The dream-sprite has led him, by spell of her trance,
To his once happy home, to his children, his wife,
To all that is dear or is hallowed in life.
Soft arms twine around him, he hears that loved voice,
And tiny hands clap as the children rejoice.
Let him sleep on in peace: ere another day dies,
The wail of the widow and orphan shall rise.

V.

But all are not sleeping: there's work to be done.
For when the day faded, the red, western sun

Threw beams of his glory o'er corses all pale,
And ghastly, and bloody.   The scene told a tale
That was but the prelude of suffering and sorrow,
Held back in reserve for the terrible morrow.
By kind, friendly hands was each tenderly borne
To the last, quiet rest, and those mangled and torn
Were soothed and attended.   Like phantoms of night
Seemed the slow-moving figures,—a weird, solemn sight.

VI.

Ethric sat far from the others, all bent
By weight of some sorrow, on revery intent.
For thought travels fast, when excitement impels
The mind to its flight, and all distance it tells,
While time becomes nothing, or moments as years,
When dreadful anxiety governs our fears.
He has lived, since we saw him commissioned to bear
Despatches to Jackson, through more than the share
Of excitement and danger that man oft receives.
Just now he looks rapidly back, and conceives
The fearful importance of each weary mile
So hastily travelled.   Its image the while,
Indelibly stamped on his memory and true,
Now passes before him in one grand review.
He sees the long column that Jackson has led
Begin that strange march.   Forward still, while the tread,
In a dull, heavy sound, falls again to the earth,
Never resting, nor pausing, nor heeding the dearth
Of raiment and rations.   On! on! toward the north,
Still trusting their leader, they follow him forth,
Never daring to question, for mystery deep
Round e'en the least movement "Old Stonewall" will
      keep.

Forward! through by-ways, o'er each quiet farm,
Silently, swiftly, and ere the alarm
To the foe had been given, there, far in his rear,
Like a bolt from a sky that was peaceful and clear,
Jackson fell on Manassas! As one from a dream,
Pope aroused in amazement. Afar came the gleam
And glare of the fire-fiend; in one smouldering heap
Lay the store of supplies that his army must keep.
Yet no time for resting; for still in advance
Of Lee and of Longstreet, those legions, perchance,
That turned to oppose them, might strike in their power.
Then, cautiously, swiftly, in night's silent hour,
Jackson's column was wheeled, and quick marshalled each
      rank.
By skilful manœuvring, the enemy's flank
Was soon reached in safety; and Longstreet and Lee
Had met him; his men from the danger were free.

VII.

'Twas a brilliant manœuvre. A people's wild praise
Crowned Jackson the hero of glorious days.
Behold, here, a handful of men,—weary, worn,
Hungry and foot-sore, and tattered and torn,
A Nemesis prove, as their brave leader hurls
Their strength 'gainst the might that his foeman unfurls.
While the world at his feet all its full praises cast,
Bewildered and stricken, the foe stands aghast.

VIII.

As Ethric still musingly sat, a deep awe
And dread of the morrow filled all that he saw.
There was nothing to him on the rough battle-ground
Either new or untried; for he oft had been found

Where shot rained the thickest, and brave comrades fell,
Yet know naught of danger.　To-night seemed to tell
That his fate would soon meet him.　A vague, nameless
　　　dread
The future presented.　Quick turning his head,
Half ashamed of the feeling he strove to repress,
Half longing for one to whom all to confess,
He saw that a soldier was watching him there:
Their eyes met an instant, and all the deep care
Of the moment was gone in the joy to extend
His hand once again to his old college friend.

IX.

HASTINGS.

Why, Ethric! you here?　I began to suspect
That time-honored legends that man will reject
When his childhood is over, were true, and your ghost
Was meeting me here.

　　　　　Ethric laughed, while the host
Of fancies his dreamings had conjured up rose
Like ghosts of his making.

ETHRIC.

　　　　　'Tis I.　That repose
Which many are seeking, ere facing the clash
Of arms on the morrow,—that sleep which can dash
Forebodings away,—has from me wandered far.

EDWARD.

Thus causing our meeting, the first since the war.

ETHRIC.

The first; but the tumult, the crash, and the roar,
Though working their ill, cannot touch the heart's core

Where friendship is safe. This is not my command ;
I am here on a mission. When Stuart's bold band
Had captured those papers that warning gave Lee,
He sent me to Jackson : it seems only he
Could make that bold march on the enemy's flank.
A courier detained, thus I fell in this rank,
And have made the long march with these men who are
     strangers.

EDWARD.

To find your old friend at the end of its dangers.
What think you of Jackson ?

ETHRIC.

             A leader most rare,
Who loves with his men every peril to share.
This struggle will crown with bright laurels his name,
Yet none ever lived more indifferent to fame.
His instant decision great genius proves ;
For, seeking no counsel, reliant he moves,
Nor looks for disaster. " Napoleon believed
In his star ;" in the same way, success is received
By Jackson as destiny.

EDWARD.

            Ay ! Through the line
His faith is contagious. Though battery or mine
Lay masked at the feet of his men, o'er them all
They would recklessly charge, did his loved voice call.
He knows their devotion, and trusts it full well,
And is stirred to the soul by their weird-sounding yell.

ETHRIC.

Lives in my memory one night at tattoo
(The first that I reached him), his form came in view.

Gave the near ranks the yell, and each quick answer made,
Line back to line, and brigade to brigade,
Through division and corps, till the forests rang out,
And loneliest echoes were caught in the shout.
Jackson, uncovered, stood still near his tent,
And eagerly listened the cry that was sent
Over woodland and hill, till the answering strain
Had died in the distance; then caught up again
Like echoes it came.   Leaning forward to hear,
Intent that the last, dying note reached his ear,
In silence he stood.   When the full hush had come,
Unbroken by aught save the roll of the drum,
He turned to his tent; but 'twere easy to tell
He loved as sweet music that unearthly yell.

EDWARD.

I have seen him in camp when the day's march was done,
Surrounded by men who had victory won,
Hat in hand, 'neath the trees, kneeling there on the sod,
Leading in prayer to his Maker and God
The battle-scarred veterans whom he had led
To mouth of fierce cannon, o'er dying and dead.
Ay, I have seen men with the cards in their hands,
Mayhap with an oath on their lips, group in bands,
With uncovered heads, and wait silently there,
And reverently listen to Old Stonewall's prayer.
Had one jest been uttered, or one scoffing word,
That instant had burst forth the love that was stirred,
And men who, perchance, for themselves would not pray
Had taught the rash scoffer to heed Stonewall's way.
For we know him sincere; and we follow through fire
That leader in faith, that his faith can inspire.

And we know when in store is some terrible fight.
As the rank filed in place, did you watch him to-night ?
He sat on his horse with his slouched hat pulled low,
And his right hand was raised, and his lips moving slow.
There is wild work ahead ; for throughout his command
Every man notes with awe Jackson's uplifted hand !

ETHRIC.

Have you been with him long ?

EDWARD.

          Yes ; through many a battle,
In advance and retreat, 'mid the war's wildest rattle.
At Manassas, last year, 'twas his men held the tide
Of battle for hours.   Then, marking the wide
Line of Blue o'er the hill, quick the battle to change,
He held in our fire for work of " short range ;"
And we gave them the bayonet.   " Thus my brigade,"
Said Jackson's report, " by God's blessing was made
The Imperial Guard."   And the morrow will show
That brigade in its place !

ETHRIC.

          Let us trust each may know
His place and his duty.   Were you in the Valley ?

EDWARD.

Yes ; early in May, Jackson bade the line rally.
He drove Banks before him, and captured the town
Of Winchester, wreathing with greater renown
The name we adored.   His retreat grandly covered,
While Fremont and Shields on his right and left hovered,

Each able to crush him, must ever remain
Enrolled 'mongst the brilliant achievements whose chain
Is dear to the South.

ETHRIC.

Even that bore its shade.

EDWARD.

Ay! a great one.   The gloom Turner Ashby's loss made
Was felt through the land.   Gallant, noble, and brave,
His life proved his love for the cause he would save.
A thorough Virginian, he clung to the past,
And the long-hallowed memories time had there cast
Round the flag of the Union.   Once finding all lost,
He shrank not a moment from suffering or cost,
But opposed the old flag when he found that it threw
Protection o'er creeds he denounced as untrue.

ETHRIC.

Were you there when he fell?

EDWARD.

                    Yes; I ne'er shall forget
The scene to my mem'ry so vivid as yet.
'Twas Ashby's famed cavalry guarded the rear
Of that wondrous retreat.   Came the enemy near,
And two infantry regiments quick were sent back
To act with his cavalry meeting attack.
The foe lay concealed under cover of fence;
Our regiment burst on the ambush from whence
Came a fierce sheet of flame; he, unhorsed by the fire,
Sprang forward,—seemed danger his soul to inspire.

Waving his sword, "Chârge, Virginians!" he cried.
A rifle was heard, and that instant had died
Virginia's loved son.   But a few yards away
From the marksman who killed him his dead body lay.

ETHRIC.

Through long years to come shall his name honored live ;
And Virginians just tribute his memory will give.
There are names now enrolled in the lists of our dead
Whose chivalric virtues pure, bright halos shed.
There are more yet to come, reaping full shares of glory.
And who shall be next ?   But you paused in your story.

EDWARD.

Jackson safe from the Valley, the campaign was done,
The Federal plans broken, fresh victories won.
Snatching sleep in his saddle, he followed on down
Where Richmond lay trembling beneath the dark frown
Of the hosts of McClellan.   Those struggles you know,
Where blood freely marked Chickahominy's flow.

ETHRIC.

Those were terrible days, yet they proved Southern worth
And heroic devotion to the land of our birth.
Yet again were we safe, and our loved city shielded,
And the enemy stunned 'neath the blow that was wielded.

EDWARD.

Ay, stunned, but not crushed ; for as yet, while the smoke
Of those battles ascended and wild echoes broke,
Jackson's army had wheeled, and ere long Slaughter's
        Mountain
Came quick on the roll,—where our blood like a fountain

Gushed as an offering noble and grand
From true Southern hearts to the loved Southern land.
In that fearful struggle our first line was shattered;
Another pressed on, and ere long it was battered,
Then halted, and wavered, and reeled from its place,
As the foe hurled the storm of hot shell in its face.
'Twas an age in a moment, but Jackson was there;
And soon was that faithful sword flashed in the air;
And when Stonewall was known to be leading the van,
In the once broken line he recalled, not a man
But was certain of victory. With wild cheer and shout,
We rushed to the charge, and dismay and quick rout
To the enemy followed. The rest you can trace.
Yet strange that we met not, till here on the place
Where that march has its climax. Manassas' old glory
Must soon be revived, thus to finish the story.

X.

ETHRIC.

God pity the dear ones at home who shall weep
For the soldiers to-morrow who sleep their last sleep!
Edward, to you, as my tried, trusted friend,
There is much I would say. Dull forebodings extend
Their sway o'er my thoughts, and the gloom that I feel
Hovers darkly round all things, o'er all seems to steal.
I have laughed at presentiments, held in derision
The thousand devices and careful precision
Which men have adopted from some treasured store
Of some time-worn tradition or legend of yore;
Yet to-night there's a still voice speaks in my heart
And whispers my fate. And anon I will start;
For before me there rises a sad, tender face,
Where grief and anxiety each leave their trace;—

And the eyes mutely pleading my soul fill with dread.
You remember Theon?—Like a hope that is dead,
Her face comes before me. I know that some sorrow
Hangs over her pathway. 'Tis not wise to borrow
More grief in the future than falls to one's lot,
But bravely meet that which one finds in each spot;
Yet, knowing our love, can you wonder I feel
This sadness when meeting those eyes' mute appeal?

XI.

(On the night's solemn stillness a slight rustling sound
Had startled the soldiers, and, glancing around,
They sought for its cause. Neither saw, 'neath the shade
Which a cluster of alders quite near them had made,
A form quickly dropped; but the wind murmured low,
And they heard there the sentinel's tramp to and fro.)

EDWARD.

Nay, Ethric, speak not in this way, for your brain
Is unduly o'erwrought. Be your brave self again.
'Tis unlike you, this fancy,—and morbid, this fear,
Unworthy your judgment or courage.

ETHRIC.

Nay, hear:
Have patience a while; let me hastily say
Even all that I wished; for ere long the great day,
So heavy with fate of our land, will have risen,
And many a soul, ere its close, from the prison
Of clay be released. Now to you, you alone
Of all those around me, my secret is known.
To-morrow my duty as courier calls
Where danger is greatest, where lead thickest falls;

And duty is honor,—and honor is life.
God pity Theon, if I fall in the strife!
Take her name and address: if my body is found,
By the holiest ties of a friend's oath be bound
To comfort her sorrow. You'll write to her there;
Send this in the letter (a lock of his hair
Ethric quickly had severed), and tell her the past
For her sake is hallowed, that, true to the last,
My heart's every beat to her memory is given;
Ay, true to the love-pledge, to country, and heaven!

XII.

(Called a dove its companion? or was it the moan
Of some wounded comrade, whose low, subdued tone
Broke the stillness again? Or perchance 'twas the sound
Of the night-watch, still pacing his long, dreary round?)

XIII.

The hair that he gave, Edward silently took,
And placed it secure in the leaves of his book;
Then sought by a tender and delicate skill
To turn his friend's mind, and these fancies to kill.
So he talked of the days of their boyhood and youth,
When, with life all before them, they pledged there the
        truth
Of pure, lasting friendship; of those they had known;
Of incidents trivial, yet that had grown
To them most important; because they had made
Those early days precious, they never could fade.
And then Edward told him his own tale of love,—
Of the maiden whose pledges around life had wove
A halo all bright, that o'er each gloom could throw
A livening ray. Then they talked long and low

Of their hopes for the future; their faith in the cause
For which they had fought; of the world's great applause
Should their freedom be won and their victory be gained,
And the rights they had cherished so long be maintained.

XIV.

ETHRIC.

The night is far spent. Mark you yonder bright star?
The bird's wakening song heralds morning afar.
The heavens bend over us calm and serene:
This evening the sun will sink low on a scene
Of bloodshed and carnage that demons delight
To see upon earth. May God grant to the right
The blessing of victory! Angels of heaven,
Watch well o'er the homes for which blood shall be given!
Let us rest while we may. Edward, keep well your oath.
This day each to duty. God watch o'er us both!

XV.

The two friends had parted. The man long concealed
Stepped forth, while the moonlight his suffering revealed,
And he moaned in his sorrow.

     " What fate led me here,
To show me the doom of a hope that was dear,
And mock at my anguish? The vision is gone,
But its memory lingers and haunts me. Theon!
Must I live on to see your devotion thus given?
Your love bless another? Long, long have I striven
This passion to kill, but it rises in might,
Defies, in its strength, stern adversity's blight,
And lives on, my one—only love. Will the morrow,
Sparing him, yet spare me to this crown of my sorrow?
My brain reels in madness! Would heaven that I,
In the fierce, coming battle, if he live, may die!"

11*

CANTO TWELFTH.

I.

THE long night was over. The first ray of light
Revealed to the watcher a gorgeous sight,—
Two armies drawn up in their hostile array,
Each eager for life-blood,—the Blue and the Gray.
The hosts reaching far on Manassas' broad plain,
Platoons being formed o'er the graves of the slain.
The bright banners waved, and the bayonets gleamed,
As o'er them the rays of the morning sun streamed.
Through the long lines came the drum's steady rolls,
Calling some to fresh laurels, and summoning souls.
All nature was smiling in freshness and beauty,
And brave men stood firm in their full sense of duty.
Some crazed, by the moment's excitement, were wild;
And others, calm, resolute,—life-passions mild,
Yet deep and unchanging;—each ready to yield
Life, fortune, and all, save a name, on the field.

II.

In the first hush of morning, some stern, sullen gun
Boomed angrily over the plain, and anon
There came from the outposts the rifle's sharp crack,
And hearts were expectant as fate held them back.
The long hours of morning wore slowly away,
When suddenly roared o'er the scene of the fray

126

A thunder so fiercely, so terribly grand
That even its echoes were felt through the land.
Another again, still the loud volley broke,
And the fair sky was blackened and shrouded by smoke,
As if pitying Nature had drawn the dark screen
In kindness men's passions and heaven between.
The battle is joined with one fearful crash,
And headlong the current is borne in its dash,
While swift rush of bullets and fearful death-cries
Float aloft on the breeze that ascends to the skies.

III.

Bravely stands the advance of the foe, while the storm
Is poured through their ranks, where full many a form
Lies low on the ground.   Seem the clustering trees
Behind them to open, and forth on the breeze
Floats the beautiful flag of another long line,
And the loud trumpets sound, and the bayonets shine.
On they come in their strength where the Old Brigade
        waits,—
On they come, falling bullets proclaiming their fates;
While the cannons of Lee, e'en as fiends in their wrath,
From chosen position are sweeping their path,
And into their ranks pour the hot shot and shell,
Each doing its work with a power that will tell;
For wide gaps are made and deep furrows ploughed
        through,
And men are piled dead in the ranks of the Blue.
Still another line comes, and that grand, fearful fire
Rolls on o'er the plain like a demon's wild ire.
They waver and falter; then rally, and turn
In last frantic effort their laurels to earn.

Yet still boom the thunders, and still that hot breath
Is scorching and raking their legions to death.
Again they have halted,—they reel and fall back,
And order is broken.   Then quick on their track,
With a wild, ringing yell, like a tiger at bay,
Then loosed in his strength and hurled forth on his prey,
Jackson's men are upon them.   The bayonets flash,
And the Southern line on in the maddening charge dash.

IV.

Through the morn, Ethric rode here and there with some
    message,
Never heeding the danger; all sense of his presage
Was gone, leaving now but the one reigning thought
That the cherished Palmetto in victory be brought
From the field of the battle.   In waiting he stood,
As the Southern rank dashed in the charge through the
    wood,
And the loud shout of triumph that rang o'er the plain
Was his signal to hasten to Lee, that the chain
Of success be prolonged.   Striking spurs in his steed,
He bounded straight on with a rocket-like speed;
Caring not that he rode on the battle's full tide,
Pausing not as he marked here and there at his side
The torn bleeding forms of his comrades laid low;
Still onward where duty constrained him to go.
As yet on the right the close sharp-shooters played
The shrill prelude of battle: he dashed through a glade,
And his mission was guessed, and a bullet quick sped,
While the riderless horse galloped madly ahead.

V.

Far away to the right stretches Longstreet's brave corps;
Its leader has scanned the great battle-field o'er,

And sees now the moment to hurl his whole rank
On the enemy's left and then round on his flank.
Then far down the line rang the loud battle-cry,
And the men hastened on, with a firm do or die
Impressed in each move,—Jenkins, Pickett, and Hood,—
On, over the hill-side,—on, on to the wood,
Forward like madmen, while each trusty gun
Is fired, and loaded again as they run.
The old " First Virginia" leads far to the right,
With now but its remnant of men for the fight;
The others have fallen on each battle-field
Since first the loud bugle did call them to yield
Their all to their country.   Even here on this plain
Full many a veteran left them is slain.
Georgians and Texans their strong support bring,
And herculean force 'gainst the enemy fling,
Which sweeps with a pow'r that no line can withstand,
And breaks in confusion each fresh-gathered band.

VI.

The loud cannons thunder, and wild the storm rages,
Writing in blood upon history's pages
Full many a tale both of valor and woe,
Full many a terrible agonized throe.
Out in the sunbeams the bright sabres flash !
On in their madness the hard bullets crash !
Shrieks of the wounded, and groans of the dying,
Clatter of horses' hoofs struggling and flying,
Shouts of the leaders, and cheers of the men,
Ring in wild concert through forest and glen.
Still press the Southrons on, bringing at length
'Gainst the enemy's line all their valor and strength,

Fighting as hot-blooded Southrons can fight
When all is at stake that their honor deems right;
Closing down on the foe, till the V, in which form
Their lines were first bared to the terrible storm,
Has oped in the centre, and right and left wings,
Under Jackson and Longstreet, o'ercoming all things,
Are pushing the enemy hard on each side,
While Lee's fatal guns leave their ranks open wide.

VII.

'Tis the crisis of battle!   That moment is heard
The loud order, " Charge !" and the clear-ringing word
Has passed like a flash down the whole Southern line.
Then up from the earth, as if some magic mine
Has poured forth its legions, the infantry spring,
Close shoulder to shoulder, while demon yells ring.
In the bright sunlight the bayonets glisten ;
On come the men, never pausing to listen,
Never shrinking a moment, nor checking their tread,
When the Northern balls plough through their ranks, and
　　　　the dead
Their bayonets drop from their powerless hands ;
Only pressing more closely in broad solid bands,
Never leaving a gap, where a comrade is slain,
On they come, like a hurricane wild o'er the plain !

VIII.

Men can stand brave hearing mad cannons roar,
And while storms of fierce bullets are sweeping them o'er ;
There is that in the sound which the human mind crazes
And makes it insensible still to the phases
Of terror surrounding, creating a joy
And thirst for the battle fear cannot destroy.

But firmly to stand and unflinchingly face
The cold, silent steel sweeping all from its place,
Like some fierce tornado from which naught can save,—
Ah! this takes a courage e'en rare to the brave.
The Southrons sweep far with that tempest of steel
The last ray of hope that their foemen may feel.
Full routed, in utter confusion they fly,
And the loved Southern banner floats proudly on high!

IX.

The great day is over; the fierce work is done,
And corses are strewn where the victory is won.
The beautiful sward on the laurel-wreathed plain
Is dyed with the blood of the mangled and slain.
Over the scene the dark curtain of night
Kind Nature has drawn, thus to shut out a sight
Whose cold, sickening horror would bid angels weep
At the depth man has plunged into sin's fearful deep.
But all is not still: here and there is yet gleaming
The light of some shell through the black darkness stream-
     ing;
Away in the distance, the faint echo comes
Of last straggling shots and the roll of the drums.
And, as it all ceases, the day with its glory
Is claimed by the past in its volume of story.

CANTO THIRTEENTH.

I.

AFTER the battle! Alas! who may know
The sorrow, the anguish, the deep sense of woe
Those few words may carry? The doubts and the fears,
The weary suspense, and the hot, blinding tears;
The hearts which the burden of grief snaps in twain
Or numbs into apathy deadening pain;
The burial of brightest hopes silently cherished,
The homes draped in black for the darling ones perished.
Great was the victory won, rich the price given;
Its echo ascends in one loud wail to heaven!

II.

By its fury unharmed, e'en as soon as the end
Of the conflict had come, Edward thought of his friend,
And made eager question, yet no tidings came.
He listened at roll-call, where name after name
Met ominous silence. He found the brigade
To which Ethric belonged, and there futile search made.
His General, remembering the courier brave,
And hearing his story, full privilege gave
To Edward, enabling him freely to gain
Information he wanted. Thus over the plain,
With his comrades detailed for the wounded and dead,
He wearily roamed, and as mournfully read

132

The lists that were kept of the sufferers who lay
In each improvised hospital. Day followed day,
Re-echoing each for the clue that he sought
Its full disappointment. Early days, fraught
With all their bright hopes and their innocent pleasures,
With blessings youth slights and that manhood deems
      treasures,
Loomed upward before him, and memory's spell
Seemed tenderly round Ethric's name now to dwell :
His free, boyish daring ; his wild, reckless boldness ;
The quiet reserve that so many thought coldness,
But which only screened from a stranger's light view
A heart warm and tender for those who were true.
Edward shuddered to think that so noble a life
Should forfeit its promise in war's angry strife.

III.

Yet train after train sped afar on its road,
Bearing onward to Richmond each suffering load
Of poor human wrecks, and yet groan after groan,
Or gasp of the dying, or piteous moan,
Or agonized pleading for succor and care,
From over the battle-field rose on the air.
In a quaint country inn, ofttimes found by the way,
Now an improvised hospital, sheltered, there lay
Those waiting conveyance. Detailed for the night
To watch while perchance Death should leave there his
      blight,
Just after the sunset, awaiting his hour,
Edward yielded himself unrestrained to the power
Of sadness : though bravely it struggled, his hope
Had yielded at last, quite unable to cope

With this constant denial. The warrior shrank
From his yet waiting duty. The courage that drank
And stimulus gained from known fountains of danger,
Sat quivering now, and was dumb, and a stranger
To all sense of action. How could he impart
The news that would bury a young loving heart
In abysses of grief? Not to-night: he would wait.
Perhaps ere the morrow some merciful fate
Would spare him this duty. The soldier's tried friend,
His pipe, was forth summoned, its good help to lend:
A sweet panacea, it comforted grief,
And brought to his mind, heavy-burdened, relief.

IV.

What strange, subtle influence, what potent charm,
What power to rescue from care and from harm,
What infinite sympathies, what silent spell,
In each little whiff of tobacco must dwell!
When the heart is oppressed, or the brain may be weary,
When sunbeams are radiant, or days dark and dreary,
When friends are around, and their presence gives birth
To scenes of festivity, gladness, and mirth,
In moments of trouble, or fits of the blues,
The weed is at hand all its aid to infuse.
Though intricate pathways with briers seem choking,
What matter? the way may be opened by—smoking.

V.

Edward walked to and fro o'er the lone country road,
The smoke curling upward, and bearing the load
Of care that oppressed him,—when sudden approach
Of wheels broke his rev'ry. Drew near him a coach,

With servants in livery, horses well cared for,
An evidence bearing of journey prepared for :
He knew it the carriage of one whose condition
In life furnished token of wealth and position.

VI.

At the inn door it paused, and the travellers descended,—
A lady in plain, heavy mourning, attended
By an elderly man. The guard having read
Their passports, they entered. With unchanging tread,
Having noted the strangers, did Edward resume
His walk and his pipe, sweetest solace in gloom.
As he passed near the guard, he inquired the name
That was borne on the passport. " Clyde Rutherford,"
    came
The guard's startling answer. Flashed over his brain
The strange lady's mission : his friend's face again
There floated before him,—seemed pleading anon
For his love, for his country. Could this be Theon?
Ere courage should fail him, he followed the thought,
And, entering the inn, the chief officer sought.

VII.

A few hurried questions, some brief answering word,
His course was decided. She could not have heard
The tale he must tell. He must see her at once ;
'Twere useless to falter ; and then for the nonce
The soldier's heart failed him and grew strangely weak.
How should he approach her ? what words should he speak—
He, a stranger—of comfort ? He thought of Estelle,
His own waiting loved one, and silent tears fell.
God spare her the anguish in store for Theon !
God grant that their life-streams through years might flow
    on !

VIII.

Using a leaf from his note-book, he wrote,
And sent to Theon, with his name, this brief note:
" Miss Rutherford, I have the honor to bear
A message from Ethric Montgomery.   Spare
One moment to me."

IX.

                    Did the moments creep past
Like hours in waiting.   Came answer at last:
In the small private office they waited to know
What tidings they could :—Mr. Hastings would go
Thither to them at once.

X.

              \   Edward entered the room,—
A dismal apartment, whose mute, clinging gloom
Pervaded all things that its boundaries enclosed.
A stately old gentleman, calm and composed,
Most courteously met him, and quietly said,
" My niece, sir, Miss Rutherford," turning his head
To the young lady near him.   Her large eyes grew dim,
And her face flushed and paled.

THEON.

                    You have tidings from him ?

EDWARD.

None since the battle ; a message before.

XI.

Then, dazed by his bluntness, his eyes sought the floor,
And quick, in confusion, were reading her face,
Now rigid as marble and bearing no trace

Of color; the pale lips were firmly compressed,
And her whole strength was brought to hear what she had
 guessed.

XII.

Seemed the moment an age. Edward dared not betray
His emotion; the thousand kind things he would say
But a short time before, now, alas! were all gone.
Still the statue moved not, only low murmured, " None !"
Like the far-carried echo of some mournful spell
Bursting forth from its silence deep sorrow to tell.

XIII.

She must be aroused, and this lethargy broken ;
Grief must assert itself, life give some token,
Or else,—and he shuddered the issue to think ;
She seemed there so helpless, yet over the brink
Of pitiful ruin,—for reason or life,
The one or the other, would yield in the strife.
What could he do? Ah! he thought now,—the hair !
He quickly withdrew it, all waving and fair,
Then silently, reverently, came to her side
And placed the soft tress in her hands opened wide.

XIV.

She started as one from a sleep, and, amazed,
Glanced at him, and then dreamily, fixedly gazed
At the curl well-remembered. With one stifled groan,
She sank in a chair, the while moan after moan
Escaped her, and then the wild torrent of tears
Flowed freely, flowed on, like the fountain of years.

XV.

Away from her side Edward slowly withdrew,
As if yielding her privacy. Grief was not new

Or a stranger to him.   Upon many a field
He had seen favorite comrades their precious lives yield;
He had seen the big tears that would stealthily creep
Over sun-hardened cheeks from eyes unused to weep;
Yet he never saw this,—and his stern spirit failed;
The soldier was conquered, the man's strength had quailed.

XVI.

At last, when the storm-burst of grief had been spent,
When the sobs were less frequent, the slight form less bent,
And an effort was seen her emotion to smother,
He approached her again as a kind, tender brother.
Then, quietly, calmly, he pictured the scene
Of his meeting with Ethric; told where they had been;
Of Ethric's last mission; his change of command;
· Of his courage, his friendship, and all the bright band
Of virtues that crowned him; and, then, of the message
He charged him to bear when o'ercome with the presage
Of some fearful ill, and some pre-ordained sorrow
That fate held in store for his love on the morrow.

XVII.

She caught at his words in her bitter distress
With an interest intense that her tears could repress;
And when he had paused, she extended her hand,
And, struggling her full, steady voice to command,
She answered him sadly:

XVIII.

THEON.

I thank you.   His friend
Shall also be mine; for your oath is at end.

" True to the love-pledge!" Ay, true to the last;
Those few words recall me to life, for the past.
Suspense is not hopeless. Until he is found,
Pale, silent, and sleeping, unheeding all sound,—
Until I have stood by his newly-made grave,
My trust shall assert the rich boon that I crave.
This faith shall sustain me; this hope shall still guide
Through all intervening, till safe at his side
The "love-pledge," unbroken, be uttered once more,
And grief will be banished, and doubt will be o'er.
Until Ethric comes shall each moment be given,
In echo of him, to my country and heaven.
Our fair Southern land will have need of each one
Of her sons and her daughters. There's work to be
    done,
There are foes to be fought, there is succor to send,
There are homes to be saved, there are rights to defend.
Ay, and more than all this: comes the urgent appeal
For woman's own work ! Must the heart be of steel,
Unmoved that can hear through our country the cry
That summons her daughters. The days are gone by,—
The days of our dreaming,—their visions are fled,
And bitter realities round us are spread.

XIX.

MR. RUTHERFORD.

Her sons will more bravely march on to the slaughter,
Remembering the courage of each Southern daughter,
The suffering, the patience, heroic and true,
That tells to the world all that woman can do.
May He who rules all things in heaven and earth
Look down in compassion, behold all the dearth

That war's cruel legions have left in their tread,
The lives that are darkened, the hearts that have bled,
And, meeting the storm with omnipotent will,
Hush the tempest of wrath with His grand " Peace, be
      still !"

CANTO FOURTEENTH.

I.

Far away from the land of the orange and palm,
From the clear Southern skies, and the tropical calm,
Where the wild winds anon rush abroad in their power
And scatter their blight over forest and flower,
Where sternly the ice-king his chill sceptre wields,
And covers with mantles of snow the green fields;—
Far away in a lone Northern prison, whose wall
Defiantly rose in its strength; where the call
Of loved ones could reach but in echo of heart,
Lay veterans, weary and worn; for each part
Had nobly been played, and full many a scar
Gave evidence now of their valor in war.

II.

There were men strong in health, and their stout hearts
    would yearn
For blessings of freedom, and power to spurn
Restraints that withheld them; and others, who lay
Prostrate with disease that asserted its sway,
Would moan in their anguish for some tender hand,
Some loved one afar in their own Southern land,
To bathe the hot brow, and to soothe the wild pain
That tortured unceasing the fever-racked brain.

III.

Low down in the line of those wounded and ill,
Lay a worn, wasted wreck, bearing evidence still

141

Of a strong stalwart man, and the meaningless gaze
Of the large deep-blue eyes told too plainly the maze
That delirium brought.   The poor sufferer tossed
And turned in his anguish, the while his mind crossed
O'er the dark, misty span of a few passing years,
And wakened their phantoms of hopes and of fears.
Now in the battle he heard the loud roar
Of fierce cannonading, whose sound, as of yore,
Would rouse him to frenzy the wild shock to meet;
Then, eager the on-coming foemen to greet,
And strong in the maniac's power, he waved
His arms in defiance, as madly he raved.
Again, he was lonely, and begged for his home,
For his friends, for Theon; she had promised to come
Whene'er he should need her, and pledge the great vow
To give her the right above others; and now
She truly was needed; no other could touch
His hot brow so lightly; he wanted so much
That dear, gentle voice, whose memory could urge
Him on to his duty.   And then the swift surge
Of emotion would master his long-wasted frame,
And tears freely flow.

IV.

They had wondered his name,
For nobody knew.   On the leaf in his book,
Which the picket who captured him carefully took
From his pocket, were only the letters " E. M.,
" From Theon," and the rest, though the trace of the pen
By delicate hand was discerned, was all blurred
With gore from the wound which his daring incurred.
A messenger marked, in the rich hope to gain
Important despatches, from that fearful plain

They carried him wounded, thence hurried him on
Over rivers and bound'ries, and sun after sun
Had risen and sunk in the clouds in the west,
While tossing he lay in delirious unrest.

V.

Fellow-prisoners there heard with many a sigh
Of compassion his ravings, and low, restless cry
For her whom he loved ; and anon there were those
Around him, though numbered in ranks of his foes,
Whose memories cherishing homes that were fair,
And dear waiting loved ones they sheltered, could share
The grief of their prisoner. Courage, when true,
Right gladly and quickly all homage will do
To aught of its kindred, and hearts that are brave,
Are hearts that when tried, fullest sympathy gave
To helpless appealing.

VI.

'Twas hard thus to die
Unknown amid strangers. They fancied the cry
Of anguish Theon's broken spirit would give,
And marked that he strove for her dear sake to live ;
And in kindness they used the loved name as a word
Whose magical potence would check, when 'twas heard,
His wildest of ravings.

VII. .

Days wearily rolled,
And weeks had been counted, ere yet was controlled
The fever that wasted and burned him ; and then,
Even memory wavered and wandered, and when
He strove to recall it there came but the maze
Of intricate dreamings ; and slowly the haze

Was lifted and scattered: came scenes of the fight,
His duty as courier; then the delight
With which he had caught up the mad, joyous shout
That rang down the line, thus announcing the rout
Jackson's charge had accomplished; the full-bounding glow
Urging onward his ride, that his General should know
The glorious tidings—a quick, fearful crash—
And into his brain the hot blood seemed to dash!
Like the link of a dream came the thought of the hour
When he knew he must yield to the enemy's power;
And that was the last.   Was the victory complete?
Did the Southrons press on to the utter defeat
Of the enemy's line?   What of Edward?   Whereon,
Had aught harmed his friend, for himself could Theon
Found comfort or hope?   E'en had Edward returned
Unhurt, by what possible means had he learned
Of his wound and his capture?   What anguish and care,
What fearful forebodings that verged on despair,
Theon must have known!   Ah, he shrank from the thought,
As one with a terrible agony fraught.

VIII.

With strength just returning, he wrote, " I am here,
A prisoner held.   There is reason, I fear,
To know that no tidings from me you have gained
Since the fight at Manassas.   By Jackson detained,
I served in new rank, and my fate could be told
By none that I knew, saving one.   Still and cold
He may lie on the field.   If all hope has not died,
Theon, my own loved one, your trust has been tried
By fires of suspense that will torture and wind,
Remorseless and cruel, but waning to find

New hope to consume. During weeks that are past,
Delirious, ill, I have lain; but at last
Health offers new hope, and I trust that in time,
Exchanged, I shall come to our own Southern clime;
And, ere long, haste to claim you, my darling, my wife,
Around whom shall cluster the sunbeams of life."

IX.

His heart was less heavy when safe on its way
That letter was started. Young, hopeful, and gay,
Yet with deep, earnest nature, each trouble once o'er
But left him the stronger for battling with more.

X.

There are men that we find made of steel,—quick and
　　bright,
Hearts full of emotion. The heavens' pure light
To them can be never the calm, steady glow
Of a tried, constant sun. Hope or doubt, bliss or woe,
To them is intensified,—now in the skies,
And now on the ground. Father Time, as he flies,
Will bring to them troubles. They ne'er learn to bend;
They cannot,—they break : for 'tis easier to mend
The gathered-up fragments of once-cherished treasure
Than bear the great strain of some trouble's full measure.
There are others of iron,—stern, resolute, strong,
Though fires of affliction burn fiercely and long,
Will bend to their breath with a brave will to face,
And meet strength with strength ; and thus battling apace,
Never yielding or hopeless, they learn to rely
Upon God and themselves, and all else to defy.

XI.

The iron was Ethric.   A resolute will
Supported his principles; never until
He conquered in what he believed to be right
Did he waver or falter or turn in the fight.
Never boasting of victory, he bent to no rod;
Come sorrow or sunshine, his feet pressed the sod
With tread firm and steady; save only, the shade
Of sorrows that compassed his pathway had made
A soft, darkened background, on which sunbeams fell
More brightly by contrast.   Maturely and well
He studied his pathway, and carefully read
The line of his duty, and there must he tread,
Whatever betide him; that done, he could hope
And wait in true patience, though doomed long to grope
Through tortuous ways.   And now, bidding God-speed
To the letter he wrote, that Theon should be freed
From pain of suspense, he must quietly bide
The time that would bear him at last to his bride.

CANTO FIFTEENTH.

I.

BACK again to the South; back again to the fields
Where the grim sword of battle the war-demon wields;
Through the long, weary weeks full of suffering and toil;
Past streams of red blood that run deep in the soil;
Past groans of Antietam, and Perryville's roar,
And the echoes of Corinth that roll the land o'er;
Past it all, through the dark months of winter, that bring
New life and new hope with the opening spring.

II.

The scene is a room, richly furnished and rare,
In a far Southern home.   Wealth and labor and care
In full lavish waste leave their traces around;
In every appointment rich luxury is found.
Yet all is precise and in martial array;
E'en the chairs seem to form, as it were, a drill-day.
No birds and no flowers, no stray magazine,
No half-opened work-basket there to be seen;
In dismal formality stateliness dwells
Around all, and a marked lack of cosiness tells
Of the absence of woman, whose presence crowns home
With attractions preventing e'en one wish to roam.
Alone 'mid the grandeur, a gray-haired old man,
Whose brow is deep-furrowed ere yet reached the span
Of years here allotted.   Just now some thought weighs
And oppresses him sorely: anon his stern gaze

147

Is fixed on the window, anon on a letter
Which he slowly re-reads, as if hoping a better
Conclusion to reach.   We will read it with him.

III.

" Far away from the battle-smoke, making all dim,
Far away from the poor, mangled forms, and the gaunt,
Suffering faces whose images follow and haunt,
My mind seeks a respite and longs to take flight
And bear me to your sheltering pity to-night.
Could you know, O my uncle ! the bitter distress,
The suffering, the sorrow, the wrongs to redress,
The hearts that are bleeding, the spirits once brave
That crushed and all-powerless wait for the grave,—
Could you see, as I see, e'en from youth to old age
The one mournful story impressed on the page
The future will read,—could you hear the low wail
That comes from stanch purpose to die but not fail,—
Ah, then would you wonder a respite I seek
In the arms of your love ?   Am I foolishly weak ?
God forbid !   I am strong !   True, the woman would fly,
Yet the cause of her terror bids woman defy
Its effect and still brave it ; and therefore I stay
At the post of my duty.   Pray God send the day !

" Again o'er our land has the wild tempest broke,
And from Chancellorsville comes the dense cloud of smoke,
Which lifted reveals there a victory grand ;
Yet hushed be the murmur of joy through the land !
For lifeless and cold lies the leader whose name
Is indelibly fixed on the tablets of Fame,
Wreathed round with immortelles and covered with glory,
And linked in the chain of the legends and story

That throws o'er the South all the thrilling romance
Pertaining to old days of knighthood and lance.
Through long-coming years in which Jackson shall sleep,
Will hearts of his countrymen tenderly weep,
And childish lips quiver, and beaming eyes glisten,
And cheeks glow with fervor, as little ones listen
To tales that their sires and grandsires shall tell
Of the hero who fought for his country and fell.
More lasting than marble, such monuments these;
His work is well done.   Let him ' rest 'neath the trees !'

" To Richmond the wounded and suffering were brought,
And waiting their coming were ladies who sought
Their needs to supply.   With stores without stint,
Bandages, cordials, and linens, and lint,
From all sides they came.   And was scarcely a face
Where fearful anxiety left not its trace,
Save here and anon where a settled despair
And deep mourning dress told of war's havoc there.
For these were the sisters, and mothers, and wives
Of men who in battle formed bulwark of lives.

" Full many a shattered and pale, bleeding form,
The ruins of manhood, the wrecks of the storm,
Arrived on the train, were consigned to the care
Of friends who had anxiously waited them there.
The ordeal was fearful ; the faint heart would turn
In horror away, and the blinding tears burn.
There was no moment for pausing, nor shrinking ;
The death-fiend was busily, greedily, drinking
Life-blood of our heroes ; and willing hands went
To the work of relief, and brave, true women bent
O'er their mangled defenders, in mute tenderness
Which in its strong eloquence told their distress.

" I passed down the line, and my thoughts wandered fast
To the homes where the dark, dreary shadows were cast,—
To the Mother who heard of the victory won
And prayed in wild anguish, ' God spare me my son !'—
To the Wife who had passed through the long, sleepless
　　　　night,
Seeing naught but her Husband exposed to the fight,—
To the Maiden who trembled in fear for her lover :
The black clouds are heavy and angrily hover,
And fierce, vivid lightnings all over them flash,
And where the bolt falls, there the terrible crash
Betrays the great ruin.　O God ! my heart bled
In grief of its own, and for those who must tread
The path I have trodden.　And thus sadly musing,
With the old baffled hope every new face perusing,
My revery was broken ; for there on my way
The men had just placed a new cot, whereon lay
Edward Hastings, dear uncle, my own Ethric's friend ;
One arm crushed and mangled.　My cry seemed to send
A thrill of emotion that passed o'er his frame
In visible tremor.　I called him by name,
And he gave me a look of such mute, intense pleading
As if his deep soul were my own response reading,
While his pale compressed lips struggled something to tell.
My ear, bending low, caught the one word, ' Estelle,'
And the wish was revealed.　There was one who had power
To woo him to life,—lived a maiden whose dower
Of love was his all.　'Twas the cry of her heart
That, echoed from mine to his own, made him start.
He knew all the tale of my desolate sorrow,—
Was my fate in store for his love on the morrow ?
In his pocket I found, kept with tenderest care,
Her name and address, and I wrote to her there

And urged her to haste. When to-day she had come,
There were few words of question. Grief sometimes is
    dumb,
And the heart that has suffered is swifter to heal
Like wounds of another. One grief made us feel
Bound closely together; one grief has laid bare
Every thought that was hid in our hearts, rankling there;
While o'er them our sympathies soft halos shed
That hide their dark edges. I quietly led
Estelle to her lover. There are those who may know
'Neath her resolute calmness the weight of her woe.

" The day sped away; came the hour when earth
Draws nearer to heaven,—the hour that gives birth
To purest emotions, and tenderly takes
The dull care away that our peacefulness breaks.
That hour to-day gave a picture of bliss,
Yet subdued by its sadness. Where light breezes kiss,
Full many a form that is fevered and racked,
And many a face where the suffering is tracked,
By the side of a cot kneels a beautiful girl,
And the last beams of sunset adorn each bright curl
With radiant halos. Her slight hand is clasped,
And firmly held there, as if Love, Life had grasped,
By the hand of the soldier who helpless must lie
Supported by pillows. The echoes that die
With the hush of the day, tremble soft as each vow
Is slowly repeated that binds their hearts now,
And they twain are made one. As the minister bends
In sweet benediction, as one voice ascends
From each hardy soldier a blessing most dear ;
Not a heart but is touched, not an eye less a tear !

" With the bride's loving kiss as yet warm on my lips,
I have come from that room e'en as one who but sips
Of the full cup of joy but to find that the draught
Was meant for another, by another is quaffed.
My heart almost sinks.　Will each hope turn to pain,
And each weary search prove, alas! but in vain?
Is there no glimmering light that can herald the dawning?
No end of the night, and no birth of the morning?
Yet, heaven be praised, though I've suffered and wept,
Though bowed 'neath the gloom, has a Father's love kept
My heart keenly strung in accord with another.
Sharing her hope with Estelle, I can smother
And hide each regret that my own winding path
Lies still in the darkness 'neath full clouds of wrath.
I have sat in the school-room of grief and perceived
The load of each care is made less and relieved
Not so much by assistance that others extend
As that which is given some suffering friend.
The diamond reflects the bright light that it borrows;
Thus we, in the heat of our trials and sorrows,
Receive the rebound of our sympathies given,
The echo of that which the soul craves from heaven.

" So a fervent God bless both the bridegroom and bride!
Yet my heart shrinks in fear: will the morrow betide
Blight or hope to them both? Will the cold hand of Death
Pluck the joy from their lives, and his stern, icy breath
Freeze the fresh-blooming flowers, whose gentle perfume
Pervades all things now, giving cheer in their gloom?
God knows!　Ah! our country hath need of the brave,
Hath need of true men and true women to save
All that is dear to us, all that we cherish,
Without which the name that we prize so must perish.

.　　.　　.　　.　　.　　.　　.

" Edward will live, and ere long they will go
To their home and to happiness; I, to the woe,
To the suffering, and toil, and anxious suspense,
Praying God for the light,—praying God call me hence
Should the light be denied me. My hope must be sure;
My life shall prove Ethric what love can endure.
Yet, oh! there are times when the tempest beats wild,
I long so to come, as a weak, trembling child,
And rest me secure on your fond, faithful heart;
But duty commands me, and, true to my part,
I remain here, and He who in mercy looks down
Will lighten the cross and at last give the crown,
If not in this life, in the one far beyond
That awaits us when this life is over.

" THEON."

IV.

That was the letter; and over and over
Clyde Rutherford turned it, then gazed at the cover,
As if around that seemed each point to revolve
Which he sought by unveiling, the question to solve.
The world called him stern, uninviting, and cold;
Could the world the deep secrets he treasured unfold,
It would find buried far in his heart's sacred tomb
A memory of days in whose light, ere the gloom
Of his fate fell around them, his life had reposed.
A fair, graceful form hovered there, and disclosed,
By some hidden influence, some subtle spell,
The strength of the love that in man's heart may dwell.

V.

There came a dark day, and his one love was buried
In the grave of the past. No one knew the light hurried

From his young life had left it all blighted and scared,
Nor guessed the sad memories that love had endeared.
The bright, happy youth had emerged from the storm
With the strength of the man, and a veteran's form
Erect in defiance of destiny's wrath,
Heeding naught that impeded his straightforward path.
There were no lingering traces his grief to define,
Save the early gray hairs and the deep-furrowed line
That hardened his features; no murmur or moan
Told the world of his sorrow: he faced it alone.
But a beautiful image was hidden from sight,
And a ring that ere long should his sacred troth plight;
While men had turned coldly aside, knowing naught
But the sudden reserve which his sorrow had brought.

VI.

Time had passed on, and the heart that had braved
Its suffering in silence at last roused and craved
Some pure, helping love to rewaken the past,
Some object round which all its treasures to cast;
And the stern man had found in his beautiful niece
An angel that saved him and taught his soul peace.
From days of her childhood, at first as by stealth,
And afterwards boldly, the long-hidden wealth
Of prisoned affections around her was thrown;
And their strength with the maiden all hallowed had
    grown.
Now, the old man clung tenderly, helplessly there,
As if he well knew that, alone, she could bear
His heart far away from the frozen abyss
Into which he had plunged to the sunlight's warm kiss.
When he heard from Theon of her heart's wakened treasure,
His bountiful love would have heaped the full measure

Of bliss for her life. When the great sorrow fell,
He well knew the anguish her own heart could tell.
But hope dies with age, and to him the dark cloud
Had seemed from the first to be love's fatal shroud.
Yet, acting in sympathy then with her grief,
And knowing that action is sorrow's relief,
He had followed her on 'midst the wounded and ill,
And helped her in labors of kindness until
Some duty had summoned him home.

      And Theon,
Still nursing her hope, seeking tidings thereon,
Had pleaded in Richmond with friends to remain;
Clinging yet to the scenes that were burdened with pain,
That, for Ethric's own sake, should he never return,
Some suffering one from her own hand might learn
Woman's place in the cause. There were many had known,
And many had blessed her for kindnesses shown.

VII.

Could he, as her guardian, allow her to spend
Her life for a hope that must hopelessly end?
Was he right to sit quietly by, while the bloom
Of her bright youth sank slowly in sorrow's dark tomb?
Yet how could he call her from sense of her duty
And rouse her young heart in its spring-time of beauty
Without crushing all? And if Ethric should live,
And, returning, the proof of fidelity give,
He would here hope to find her. 'Twere cruel to take
Her heart from the work that for Ethric's own sake
She would finish, and even more cruel to hold
Her life where its tale would soon briefly be told.

VIII.

In his mind there was not even one lingering doubt
But Ethric was dead.   He would have her without
The long chain of circumstance twining around,
Inviting to search where no clue could be found.
He would have her away from the tumult and strife,
Away from the round of monotonous life
She was leading.   He wanted by tenderest care
And change her young mind, long so burdened, to bear
To its needed repose.   He would wander far back
Through the legends of ages, and mark there the track
Of by-gone years' footsteps, and, seeking gay voices,
Woo her to places where pleasure rejoices.
Thus reclaiming her life, he would see the glad smile,
Youth's dearest possession, long banished the while,
Re-enthroned on her face, and would mark the light tread
Once again as she walked.   Then an answer he sped
Announcing his coming to bear far away
His floweret from darkness to life-giving day.
Ah ! we plan in our wisdom and oft weave a snare
Whose meshes entangle the hopes we build there.

CANTO SIXTEENTH.

I.

To Richmond we turn !—city first in the thought
Of foe and defender; 'gainst which has been brought
The power of armies whose praises have filled
The civilized world ; for whose sake has been spilled
Blood that was rich, because given in love,
Unswerving devotion and constance to prove.

II.

Here have come tender women, great burdens to share,—
The mothers and wives of the soldiers who bear
The brunt of the battle,—and couches quick spread
Receive from the conflict who suffered and bled.
But the bare, wooden floors, and each lone, cheerless room,
Suggestive of want in its deep, chilling gloom,
And long, dreary rows of the scant-covered cots,
Form a desolate scene to the men whose past lots
Were luxurious ease.   Yet in keeping they stand
With the keenest privation now felt through the land ;
For labor, and hardship, and suffering, and woe,
Are words whose full meaning these people could know.
The maidens and wives who had lovingly wrought
Bright banners of silk, which they charged should be
    brought
Wreathed with victory home,—who had cheered with a
    smile
The new-forming legions, still keeping the while

Their breaking hearts still,—now, alas! felt no need
The bright smile to assume, and the buoyant " God speed!"
Had died on their lips.   In their stead, through these years,
There were black, clinging robes, saddened faces, and tears,
And the banners that waved in their beauty and grace
Were riddled and faded, blood-stained, but in place.
Yet closer they drew,—husbands, sons in the field,
Wives and mothers at home; not a heart that would yield.
In battle the phalanxes formed over graves;
At home prayed the women to heaven that saves,
Nor prayed only, but worked.   Slightest hands, that had
      done
Only daintiest tasks, now essayed, one by one,
All duties severe.   Lives of indolent ease
Became lives of working.   Such women were these,
Who, perchance, by the graves of their slain having shed
Life's bitterest tears, now heroically tread
Their dark, lonely paths,—stanching blood in its flow,
Dressing wounds with a touch only women can know,
Quivering not at the bayonet's trace,
Through long, solemn hours of night still in place,
Like ministering angels.

III.

                    And here is Theon,
Living yet in her hope, winning blessings thereon
By duties of kindness.   Her sorrow has told
Its tale in her face, and the light step of old
Is weary and slow; while the sweet voice, that brought
By its own merry sound kindred pleasure, is fraught
With heaviest sadness, and seems to reveal
What her quiet reserve ever seeks to conceal.

Yet her story goes forth, and full many a prayer
From those who are grateful for tenderest care
Has ascended to heaven with blessing o'erladen
For the dearly-loved, sorrowful, resolute maiden.

IV.

To-day from her path fled the one cheerful beam
Which in long months of darkness appeared a bright dream,
For Edward had gone with Estelle. To the last
She had kept her composure, that no shadow cast
From her life to their own might their happiness mar;
She had said the " Good-by," and the old ugly scar
Had opened again, and was bleeding once more,
And the night of her gloom settled down as before.

V.

In silence she stood till the sound of the wheels
Had died in the distance,—in silence that feels
Its own heavy burden ; then, clasping her shawl,
She turned from the house, as if fleeing from all
The sad, tender memories that dwelt o'er the place,
And the suffering and woe that she dared not then face.
Wearily, listlessly, wandering on
Through the various streets of the city whereon
The surging throng passed, she had wended her way
To the home of her friend. There are hours in life's day
When the mind, heavy-burdened, demands its repose,
And seeks renewed strength that full quiet bestows.
She longed in her room to relive the bright years,
And weep o'er their memories pure, loving tears.
She had learned the full worth of those dear, peaceful
    hours
In which were conned lessons increasing her powers

Of noble endurance,—how freely was given
The aid of a pitying, all-seeing heaven
In times of worst trial; and oft she had felt
The measure of love with each blow that was dealt.
Seeking this quiet, she passed through the door,
Then paused where she stood, as if bound to the floor,
As voices reached her.　Her friend called her name:
She answered like one in a dream.　O'er her frame
A quick shiver ran.　At this time above all
That presence woke words that 'twere pain to recall:
" For the storm may roll back in its force on your head,
And the lightnings avenge me the love that lies dead."

VI.

Not once since that evening had Harold been back;
For the changing events that had rolled in the track
Of years intervening had drawn them apart.
To-day, of all others, his presence a dart
Seemed to pierce her soul through, and she turned back
　　　　aghast
From truth of the present and scenes of the past.

VII.

As she answered his greeting, his piercing black eyes
Marked her colorless face with painful surprise;
And he spoke to her gently:

MORTON.
　　　　You are weary; rest there.

And he wheeled for her service his own cushioned chair;
And then, as if feeling her need for repose,
With that grace of good-breeding which silently throws

Such charm o'er possessors, he turned once again,
To their hostess, and quietly caught up the chain
Of their checked conversation :—the battle just fought ;
Jackson's death, and the gloom it had everywhere brought ;
The hopes of the people, their courage and will ;
And like kindred topics suggested,—until
Their hostess, called out, left the two there alone,
And each knew the other recalled memories gone.

VIII.

Harold turned to her then as he did on that night
With the same searching look, as if reading aright
Her soul's inmost thought.

IX.

HAROLD.

I have not as yet heard
What I longed most to hear.   Have you no welcome word
Henceforth to be treasured ?

THEON.

The years that bestow
Their lessons of sorrow oft check in their flow
Glad words we have spoken ; and friendship relies
On action, not language.   A perfect surprise
Your visit to me.

HAROLD.

E'en surprise may command
Some form of expression.   There are few who can stand
The arduous duties that you have assumed ;
Unless care be taken, the spark that illumed
The body with life, unprotected will perish.
Is it not also duty one's own life to cherish ?

THEON.

This work must be done.

HAROLD.

    That is true; and your name,
Where'er you have been, is enshrined in a frame
Of merited praise.　But your cheeks wan and pale,
Contrasted with you in the past, tell a tale
Of strength overtasked, of devotion that shares
A martyr's quick grave.　Cannot these pressing cares
By others be borne?

THEON.

    There are none more than I
Who require activity.　Work must supply
Vitality needed.

HAROLD.

   Dear lady, I plead,
Not alone by the right of the friend that you need,
But by one that is holier!

THEON.

    Sir!　You forget
The time and the place when ere this we last met.

HAROLD.

Nay! hear me a moment!　The love that I brought
Long ago to your feet has lived on, ever fraught
With its deep, lasting pain.　I have trampled it down,
I have scourged it, and mocked it, and e'en tried to drown
Its wild, haunting memories low 'neath the tide
Of fierce, raging war; yet like phantoms they glide
Evermore to the surface.　By that love's holy right,
By the strength it has shown living on through the night,

I plead with you now. Spare yourself from the task
That is thus self-imposed. Give the boon that I ask.
There are yet other ways that as surely may prove
How are cherished those memories held sacred by love.

X.

She shuddered. What meaning lay darkly concealed
Behind his strange language?

HAROLD.

          The years have revealed
Even more than I knew of the boundless control
The love that I pledged you has gained o'er my soul.
As the hope of my life, here I plead for your love ;
That alone may its hallowing influence prove.

THEON.

That love is another's, firm, sacred, and true.

HAROLD.

Ay, it was. Craving all, I would not now undo
One vow you then uttered. Their memories shall live
Untarnished and sacred. Released, you can give
To me your heart's remnant.

THEON.

          Your meaning, I pray?
What secret lies hidden 'neath all that you say?

HAROLD.

What secret? Miss Rutherford! Surely your dress
Is mourning; your pale face has told of distress.
You have wept for the dead?

XI.

　　　　　　　　　　She started and stood
Face to face with him there.　Every drop of her blood
Seemed to freeze in her veins.　Then again in her seat
She sank in her agony.　Utter defeat
To his long cherished hope in her face Harold read.
He saw in despair that the one brittle thread
To which he had clung snapped in twain.　Then awoke
His pity for her, and approaching, he spoke.

XII.

HAROLD.

Miss Rutherford, hear me : believe, had I known
Your ignorance of this, then my tongue should have grown
To my mouth ere it uttered these words.　I have been
But few days in Richmond, and here having seen
Your figure black robed——

THEON.

　　　　　　　　　　For my mother I wear
This grief-telling dress.　There was hope, not despair,
In my sorrow for Ethric.　I felt he would come,
And my heart should yet leap as it welcomed him home
After long, weary waiting.

XIII.

　　　　　　　　　That instant uprose
In Harold's fierce heart all its army of foes ;
And reckless, unheeding of all but the thought
That the love he had craved should no longer be fraught
With bliss in another, he madly went on.

XIV.

HAROLD.

Lady, listen to me.   There are times whereupon
The course of a life may be changed.   All unseen
The Fates' busy fingers may glide in between
Some hope that is dear and its fullest fruition,
While with cold, scorning laugh, like the fiends of perdition,
They mock at one's agony.   Came such an hour
In your life and my own.   'Twas when midnight's full
     power
All things had subdued, and the hosts that should sweep
O'er the field of the morrow on arms lay asleep;
When weighed and oppressed by the memories that burned,
I wandered afar from companions and turned
To a lone, quiet spot.   'Neath the shadows that played
Here and there o'er the scene, unobserving, I strayed
Near the place where two comrades in low tones conversing,
Were the hopes and the fears of the morrow rehearsing.
Your name caught my ear, and quick down in the dank
Matted weeds and the grasses, as if chained, I sank.
And there I heard all ; and the face and the form
Of him who asserted your love ere the storm
Of battle I marked.   Passed the long night away,
And the demons of war ruled supreme o'er the day.
I was mad in my anguish ; for love's fearful rage
Had indelibly fixed on my soul a dark page.
I watched him as past, on his foaming white steed,
Some message he bore at a furious speed.
I heard the quick shot,—saw him stretched on the earth ;
And the old hope was raised, and emotions whose dearth
Had left me the wreck of a man.   On the tide
Of the battle I plunged, moved by some stubborn pride,

That the life that had stood between all that I craved
And myself, being lost, that my own should be saved
By fate's shield alone.   Beneath bullet and stroke
Of the sabre I passed ; while the uprising smoke
Revealed all around me the dying and dead,
Yet all whistled harmlessly over my head ;
And I felt that the prize that I sought had been given
From his hand to my own by a fate-ruling Heaven.

THEON.

And you dare tell me this ?   Ah ! the stern, selfish will
That prompted your suit proves its mastery still.
This answer is final : to you I proclaim
My heart's full allegiance to one honored name.

HAROLD.

The love you have spurned will be offered no more ;
Yet still in futurity's unrevealed store
It cries out for vengeance ; and tears of despair
Shall prove how in vain is the hope followed there.

XV.

He haughtily bowed as he turned to depart,
But his last taunting words like some poisoned dart
In withering cruelty stung her pure soul,
And her terrible agony burst her control.
She sprang to her feet, and her pale, slender hand
By imperious gesture had forced him to stand.

THEON.

It shall not be thus !   By that hope's promised truth,
By the blessing each craved for the strong love of youth,

By the purity, strength, and endurance of love,
By its power through darkness its own light to prove,
Hear me now as I pledge still implicit my trust,   .
That the time shall yet come when, behold! from the dust
That love in all triumph and honor shall rise
And conquer each doubt which it scorns and defies!

XVI.

Harold quailed 'neath her glance. Looking full in his face,
She slowly went on :

THEON.

　　　　　To your shame, your disgrace,
The love you profess! It has proven its worth;
Disrobed of disguise, it proclaims its true birth
In your turbulent passions, where selfishness reigns,
And arrogant jealousy thralls with its chains.
For shame! for the name of the manhood you bear;
For shame! for that service whose honors you wear.
May the years that shall come open wide to your view
The laws you obey! May their lessons be true
To a course that, revealing that fierce hidden ire,
Shall save you at last from yourself as by fire!
We are parted henceforth! Heaven help me forgive
This blow you have dealt to a love that must live!

XVII.

He had gone. Ere behind him had closed the street door
She sped to her chamber, and there, on the floor,
She knelt in her grief. Seemed her desolate heart
Now utterly torn from all loved ones apart.
There, fainting, they found her; for nature could bend
'Neath the burden no longer. By next mail her friend
Had hastened this note: .

"Mr. Rutherford,
                                    Come!
Take your darling away to your own quiet home,
Where the sorrows here known and the tumult may cease,
And her poor, stormy life in its haven find peace."

CANTO SEVENTEENTH.

I.

THE long months of prison-life wearily rolled
In dull, dreary round, till the year had been told;
Each bringing hopes, proving false, yet as fair,
Till Hope was dethroned by the hand of Despair;
And Ethric, courageous and strong in the strife,
Grew restless and sad in this terrible life.

II.

Not a word from Theon was received in the year,
Not a message his lone, drooping spirit to cheer.
Had she heard of his fate? had she moaned him as dead?
He shuddered to think how her young heart had bled.
The sad face that came on the eve of the fight
Was ever before him.   In hushes of night,
When no sound was heard save the sentry's footfall,
There came like an echo her sweet, plaintive call,
As if Love would mock at the strength and the space,
That over its path as stern foes left their trace;
And, heedless of all, by the right of its name,
Assert and achieve its grand triumph and fame.

III.

Ah! ye war-prisons treasure a tale of distress,
A legend of sorrow for time to redress,
A memory of hearts slowly wasting and pining,
Of griefs that, though hidden, were steadily twining

The dark, fearful coil to crush out the life,
Only leaving one less to endure the long strife
While the rest crowded on.   Bear ye mem'ry of mirth
That was forced and unnatural, and witnessed the dearth
Of pleasure its presence was meant to conceal.
The years that pass on, and shall all things reveal,
Will unroll mournful secrets that lie hidden low,
And rewrite, oft in tears, the sad tale of their woe.

IV.

Ethric had waited till patience seemed over;
The man and the soldier were lost in the lover.
Came the maddening wish for his freedom again,
And a resolute scheme sprang to birth in his brain.
True, failure brought death; but this ling'ring suspense
Was fraught with a torture more keen, more intense
Than aught else could bring.   There were hushed, whis-
  pered words,
And ears trained to catch sounds as light as the birds
In their soft flight could make, while each resolute man
To whom he imparted his heart's cherished plan
Gave breathless attention.   The firm resolve taken,
The work they began with a strong will unshaken
By aught of the obstacles thrown in their way,
Pressing steadily on, inch by inch, day by day.
In long, silent hours, when their comrades were sleeping,
And the sentinel paced up and down, his watch keeping,
Carefully, patiently, hushing each sound,
They wrought out a slow, tedious way underground.
Hiding by day every vestige and trace
Whose presence, perchance, should give clue to that place,
Cautiously, warily, trusting, and brave,
They worked.   Hopes of freedom encouragement gave;

For life had grown brighter and dearer than ever,
Enhanced by the dangers of this rash endeavor.

V.

The days rolled along, and the time came at last,
The moment when, poised 'twixt the future and past,
Their destinies hung; and the hopes and the fears
That crowded that moment seemed rushing from years.
The night had closed down; not a sound could be heard
Within the dark walls,—not a low, whispered word.
There brave men were sleeping, who ofttimes had slept
On rough fields of battle where stars vigil kept.
Without, the same silence reigned over the place,
Save the dull, heavy tramp of the sentinel's pace.
A thousand wild questions flashed over each brain,
A thousand weird fancies came quick in their train.
Perchance, there was some silent prayer for success,
A pleading that Heaven their venture would bless.
Facing their chances with resolute heart,
They were off on the way. Heaven guide them apart
From its manifold dangers,—apart from its snares,
To the haven each seeks, e'en in half-uttered prayers!

VI.

Slowly on through the tunnel, now under the wall
That held them in durance; on, on, while that call
That through the long hours in Ethric's heart rings
Comes again from afar, and a new impulse brings.
Under the beat of the sentinel's round,
Under the outer wall, on through the ground,
Till safe from detection and screened from all sight,
Free men they come forth to the kind, shielding night.

They stopped where they stood, in the fresh, open air,
Irresistibly held by sad memories there,
When one of their number, with quick, bated breath,
" Thank God !" had exclaimed. 'Twas the stillness of death
For an instant felt there, for that utterance had swayed
The hearts of strong men, who, perchance, seldom prayed.
One cap was removed, quick another, and then
Uncovered all stood, echoed softly, " Amen !"

VII.

'Twas but for an instant; again to the world,
Again to the dangers that fate 'gainst them hurled,
Their footsteps had turned; for their goal, the fair land
Of sunshine and flowers.　But the resolute band
Could no longer be one; parting quick, they must need
Use caution and courage and vigilant speed;
And Ethric alone pledged his strength to secure
The boon that had moved him so much to endure.

VIII.

Then came the hard marches 'neath cover of night,
Scant rests in the shadows that hid him from sight;
Yet the way still was long, and his poor, tortured mind
Rushed far in its flight, while his footsteps behind
So wearily lagged.　But at last it was done;
The journey was o'er, and he stood 'neath the sun
Of warm Southern skies, and his true Southern blood
Leaped again with fresh vigor, and sent its rich flood
In joy through his veins, as the loved flag he greeted,—
The banner torn, drooping, but not yet defeated.

IX.

But the face came again, and Theon's pleading call;
And Love reigned supreme and held country in thrall.
Having reached his command and a brief furlough gained.
Yet onward he hastened, each trembling nerve strained,
Pausing not till he caught the light sound of the breeze
That played o'er the tops of the dear old elm-trees.
That sound in the past seemed like sweet fairy tones,
Yet now, as he listened, it came in low moans;
For the chill breath of Autumn had made the leaves cold,
And they rustled and fell 'neath his feet brown and old,
And easily crushed; while through forest and dell
The wind in wild strains sang their funeral knell.

X.

He shuddered.   Was this an ill-omen to meet
His hopes at the threshold with cruel defeat?
How dismal the homestead! how still all around!
He passed through the gateway; how startling the sound
Of his own hasty footstep! No motion, no stir;
No welcome extended, no traces of her.
All 'round were seen marks of war's ravaging hand
And the havoc and waste that were spread o'er the land.
The long halls were empty and echoed his tread
With a deep, hollow sound; and the memories there dead
Were made rude and harsh by the harsher and ruder
And ill-timed invasion of this strange intruder.

XI.

Ethric paused where he stood; seemed the past to possess
The power to submerge his strong heart in distress

By its holiest treasures; for sorrow and woe
O'ershadowed the scenes of a loved long ago.
The Æolian harp of man's nature is never
So daintily tuned to each breath that may sever
The string that is life as when pleasure and pain
Are blended and mingled in each passing strain,
Until each is so fully a part of the other
To stifle the pain would the sweet pleasure smother.
Then the harp moans and wails, and the melody swells,
And the soul's mighty power of suffering tells.

XII.

In the room where he last saw his loved one, the face
Which Theon brought from banishment hung in its place;
And its smile seemed to him the one welcome extended
From the spot where he thought earth and heaven were
      blended.
Each thing else as she left it,—her books, her guitar,
Her music and pictures,—dead voices that mar
Their own pleasing power,—inanimate things,
Yet imbued with strange life by the memory that brings
Her spell over all.   Was it true, or a trance?
Or the old fairy-tale where the knight must advance
Through thick dust of ages his loved one to claim,
And wake to new joy and new life in his name?   •

XIII.

She was gone!   All were gone!   Past the old homestead
      portal
The war-tide had swept everything that was mortal;
Yet the mute, stately walls in their grandeur stood there,
And their loneliness told the wild wail of despair

Which ere long must arise from a nation crushed low,
But dimly foreseeing, e'en now, the last blow.
Were the hush and the stillness of Rutherford Hall
A presage of some coming dark, dreadful pall
Which hung o'er the land, only biding its time
To crush out the life from the fair Southern clime?
Was their suffering in vain, and their sacrifice naught?
And worthless the terrible battles they fought?
Echoes from Gettysburg dismally fell
In thunders prophetic, worse evil to tell.
Ethric bowed in his agony; all that endeared
His heart to his life had the great struggle seared.

XIV.

When, list! through the stillness, from some upper room,
Like a quivering wail floating down through the gloom,
Linking present with past, came a harp's mournful strain;
And the long silent echoes were wakened again.
A woman's sweet voice a melody sang,
And spellbound he stood as the silvery tones rang:

I.

"A bountiful Heaven,
Its wisdom to prove,
To mortals hath given
The blessing of Love.
Though trampled, victorious,
No respite it yields;
Immortal and glorious,
Full power it wields.

II.

"Shielded and cherished,
  In pure, holy thought,
Till time shall have perished,
  With treasure 'tis fraught.
Through sunshine and sorrow
  Love's radiance streams;
Each ill-omened morrow
  Grows bright 'neath its beams."

XV.

The last ling'ring note trembled slowly and died;
The old hall's faint echoes like phantoms replied.
The song and the voice a new power gave
To the stillness that followed, intense as the grave.
The day was just over: the last sunbeams fell
On the brown leaves of autumn like some fairy spell,
And tinged their dark edges with bright rims of gold,
While the wind whistled by with a breath stern and cold.
In the home all-deserted, the long shadows threw
Their power as magic; strange images drew
That danced up and down on the old winding stair,
Like ghosts reawakened in revelry there.

XVI.

Ethric, roused from his revery, sprang to the door,
Determined the secrets concealed to explore,
When brushed lightly past him a woman's soft dress,
And he heard the low sob that she tried to repress.
How came she alone, whence the war's cruel storm
Passing by in its course, fraught with havoc and harm,
So ruthlessly swept every vestige of life,
And hurled it headlong in the terrible strife?

Had she loved here and suffered, or wandered by chance,
Of reason bereft, telling here life's romance?
Did a fatal charm hang over Rutherford Hall,
Like the grim sword of Damocles, ready to fall
Upon every bright hope when its full worth was known?
Came the words of her song, like a prophecy's tone,—

> "Through sunshine and sorrow
> Love's radiance streams;
> Each ill-omened morrow
> Grows bright 'neath its beams."

And they lifted his soul from the stupor of pain
Into which it had sunk when he first caught the strain.

XVII.

Recovering control, in an instant he tried
The stranger to follow. The terrace door wide
Was thrown in her flight, and her footprint he traced
On the soft yielding earth, to the woodland that faced
The lawn in the rear. Thence his ear caught the sound
Of swift carriage-wheels. Nothing else could be found.

XVIII.

An instant he stood, but the sadness returned;
For each object he saw was by memory burned
Deep, deep in his heart; and to stay on that spot,
Where war, desolation, and waste left each blot,
Were to lose all forever. The radiant light
That streamed from his heart's cherished love, the more
    bright
For the darkness around, in its pure, stainless beauty
Led him back once again to new life and new duty.

The storm was still raging in power o'er the land,
The War-King his sceptre still grasped in his hand.
He must back to the ranks till his oath be fulfilled,
And the strong love would live, though in duty was stilled
Its cry of distress; living on midst the fire
And smoke of the battles, sweet trust 'twould inspire.
Then his oath was renewed, but this time not alone
To his country; he bent himself low to God's throne,
And out in the stillness of night his heart poured
As a crushed, struggling heart only pleads with its Lord.
Then his life was repledged to the land of his birth,
And his pure, faithful love to the one who made earth
A heaven of bliss. And the wind murmured there,
And bore on its wings a soul's wakening prayer.

CANTO EIGHTEENTH.

I.

Turn, O Muse, from the homes all bereft of their pride,
From rooms where the echoes of voices have died,
From broad, princely acres in ruin laid bare,
Perchance from the ash-heaps sole relics left there;
Trace the path of the army through more than a year
Of anguish, privation, and terrible fear,
Winding its course over dark battle-fields,
Where freely the nation her rich treasure yields;
Where the Demon of War tramples hopes to the earth,
Then laughs in defiance or mocks at the dearth
That follows his tread; where the low moans and wails
Through long, future years shall re-echo sad tales;
Where dying eyes turn in their mute supplication
For nature's last needs; where the sealed revelation
In years to be opened shall fasten each woe,
By the blood that is spilled, by each terrible throe,
Upon those who with power the tempest to stay
Stepped aside in their passion and blindly made way.
The winter has passed. To defend their fair land,
Behold here a ragged and half-famished band
That plunge through the din and the roar and the rattle
And soul-sickening scenes of each madly-fought battle,
With that marked self-reliance and calmness and daring
That tells a stern fortitude e'en in despairing.
What though the horses are tied to caisson
With rope and raw-hide? Still the batteries rush on.

What though shoeless, the blood-tracks may mark their
    feet rent?
What though banners are riddled and sabres are bent?
The right arms that bear them are still strong and brave,
And the blood-tracks will dry. From the homes they would
    save
Comes many a picture of want and distress,
Of wrongs to the innocent urging redress,
Which, dreadful incentives, bid each soldier grasp
His rifle more firmly, till e'en in death's gasp,
In the stiffening hand, the old weapon defies
Where it cannot defend; for the love that ne'er dies,
The love of one's own native land holds its sway,
And over these battle-fields marks out their way
To last complete triumph? Nay! nay! Like a dream
Seems the hope they once cherished. Anon, the bright
    gleam
Of some passing victory crosses their path
Like a meteor's flash, making fiercer the wrath
Of the clouds that encompass them. Weary, yet brave,
Still longing the land they have cherished to save,
They close in the ranks with a resolute will,
Murmuring neither o'er hardship nor ill;
Setting aside all the hopes of the past,
They will die where they stand, holding back with the last,
Last atom of strength that each strong arm may wield
The foe that assails them. Historians that yield
All honor to heroes, look back and behold
A page all emblazoned with letters of gold?
Not so! But a page running on through the years,
Written over in blood and bespattered with tears,
Yet telling a story of tried, proven worth,
A story of love to the land of their birth,

A story of sacrifice, suffering, and woe,
Of veterans dying, yet facing their foe.

II.

Slowly and surely, across the loved soil,
The enemy crept in a strong, deadly coil,
Crushing the life and resources and strength,
Sweeping with sword and with fire, till at length,
Worn, wounded, and bleeding, the stricken land lay,
No longer enabled to meet the array
That marshalled against her in pitiless power;
Stern men bowed themselves to the grief of the hour.
The flag that the Southrons so proudly had borne
Was dragged in the dust, stained and trampled and torn.
Like clouds o'er the land rose the volume of smoke
From many a battle where ball and fierce stroke
Had dealt death around them. And homeless and sad,
Forth wandered the widow and orphan, scarce glad
That life still remained them, for over the grave
Of father and husband who perished to save
The rights they had cherished the wild-flowers grew;
And gone were the rights and the liberties too.

III.

While the first breath of spring floated warm o'er the land,
The faithful, devoted, and suffering band
Of Southrons—brave men who had fought to be free—
Bowed themselves in submission. The bright sword of
    Lee,—
That sword all-honored and stainless and pure,—
That sword, whose memory and fame shall endure
Through yet distant ages, when history shall greet
Virginia's loved hero,—that sword at the feet

Of the conqueror fell. Fell with it each hope
Of the dream-pictured future, whose sake bade them grope
Through the long years of trial and suffering and sorrow,
To win the great glory of Liberty's morrow.
Yet all was in vain ; for the valor and worth,
The fortune and fame of the land that gave birth
To chivalry's gems, had been staked and was lost;
The impetuous longing had paid the great cost.
And those that were left, pale and scarred, must now taste
War's bitterest wormwood ; the want and the waste,
Without that wild spell, whose delirious power
Makes sacrifice sweet for the sake of the hour
That shall crown all endeavor.

IV.

    The world, the great world,
That looked on in wonder, beheld their flag furled,
Their leaders dishonored, their brave men disgraced,
Their land from the throne of its glory displaced.
Would the world judge them rightly? Not now ; aye,
  perchance !
But as years roll along in old Time's swift advance,
And the dim mist shall gather and roll in between
The present and history, (the mist that shall screen
All truth from the darts with which errors assail,
Through whose medium the truth is reflected,—not pale,
But strong, bright, and glorious,—with power to lay bare
Every motive whose act its impression left there),
Then the world will read right. As Napoleon exclaimed,
When lifting his hat as he passed by the maimed
And bleeding who fought him on some gory field,
" All honor to courage unfortunate yield !"

So men of the future will bow to the truth
And valor of manhood; to altars of youth
Where sacrifice burned; to the peerless devotion
A people displayed to their cause set in motion.
Though the flag of the victor the laurel shall wear,
And o'er it a record triumphant shall bear,
Yet in time will all nations a full honor show
To the flag there surrendered and draped in its woe.
Let descendants of whom for that furled banner died,
And sons of the fathers who bore in their pride
The conqueror's flag, read the lesson of years,
The story of passion, the legend of tears,
And, honoring right, nobly learn from the past
How one glorious people, one nation to last.

V.

Ethric had plunged in the storm once again
With a restless excitement, as if the fierce pain
That gnawed at his heart, and could yet have no voice,
Could only be numbed on the fields where rejoice
The demons of carnage. Sad memories to still,
Of action and danger he drank to the fill. ˙
Now he turned from the scene, from the long fruitless strife,
Sick at heart with it all, with this purpose in life,—
To seek for Theon. For his oath had been kept
To his country inviolate, till all was swept
By the last crash away: now his oath to Theon,
Repledged on that sad autumn night, bade him on!
Bade him stop not to rest till the beacon-light star
Had led him to Love's peaceful haven afar.
No clue had been left marking course she had taken;
Rutherford Hall remained drear and forsaken.

He had written to Edward; the letters returned
Unopened, unanswered; again his heart burned
For the fate of his friend.   Sad, despondent, and weary,
His future seemed darkened by clouds black and dreary.

VI.

Too restless to linger, he started at last
For the home of his childhood, to which a loved past
Now tenderly called him.   The present uprose
With its stern, chilling facts, every hope to oppose.
Families were sleeping beneath the green sod,
Friends were all scattered, and strangers' feet trod
In long-hallowed places.   Anon, one could tell
How Theon, drooping, crushed 'neath the sorrows that fell
So heavily 'round, with her uncle had gone
In search of his fate; how the years had rolled on,
Crowded each with its cares, and yet no tidings came;
And the hall was deserted, and Rutherford name
Seemed a thing of the past.   Disappointed, he sought
The inn for repose, and soon lost in deep thought,
He sat in his room, tracing in the soft gloaming
Fair scenes, whence his feet had begun their wild roaming.

VII.

A tap at his door; scarcely turning his head,
Expecting the tray he had ordered, he said,
" Come in !" and relapsed into revery profound,
Nor noticed the entrance nor caught the light sound
Of the footsteps that rapidly came to his side,
Till a voice called, " Ethric !" and then the full tide
Of his blood swept his veins.

VIII.

It was Edward, grown older,
While a long, empty sleeve loosely hung from his shoulder.
But the hand that was left grasped his friend's strong and
      true,
As when he last held it; that time each one knew.
And they sat them down there, e'en as two from the dead,
Those men who had trodden life's way where were shed
Life's sunbeams most scarcely,—who each for the other
Had mourned with the love one may feel for a brother.

IX.

Hastily passing his own prison-life,
His illness, escape, and return to the strife,
Ethric quickly, with all the true zeal of a lover,
Besought his old friend the lost clue to discover.
And he sat with his head buried low on his hands,
And forced all control that a strong man commands,
While Edward told all :—

X.

Of Theon's deep distress,
Which haunted his mind, when he strove to repress
His evil forebodings on that dreadful night
Preceding the day of Manassas' wild fight.
How he, Edward, met her; her agony there,
And passionate grief o'er that one lock of hair;
Her faith in the future, and trusting reliance,
Which, waiting for Ethric, set doubts at defiance.
Of the long, noble work that had followed her vow,
And which many a witness could summon, e'en now,
From those who had suffered; and of his own wound,
And sympathy tender Estelle had there found

16*

In Theon's gentle heart.   Ethric tried to conceal
The tears o'er his face that would silently steal,
As Edward told more.   Of the cheek growing pale,
And the steps less elastic, while sorrow's full tale
Was betrayed by no murmur, no shrinking from duty,
But borne with endurance heroic in beauty.
Of her meeting with Harold, the blow he had given,
'Neath which her brave heart had all faithfully striven,
In holiest trust, that their joint, answered prayer
Would bring back her lover, to wait for him there.
Then he told of her uncle's alarm and concern,
Lest, harassed by suspense, when at last she should learn
By hope's full denial the truth that he feared,
She would sink 'neath the blow, and her fair young life,
        seared,
Should lay itself down in the last quiet sleep,
As nature refused greater sorrow to keep.
How he bore her away, like a delicate flower,
To cherish and nurse in some sheltering bower,
Till youth should recall its bright spirits and bloom,
And mock at the fate that would hie to the tomb.
Then he told how he promised Theon, ere she sailed,
To press with the search till the last clue had failed
Or success been achieved; how she left the assurance
Of love all-abiding in steadfast endurance;
How letters anon o'er the ocean were brought,
Giving trace of their wand'rings, with old questions fraught.
Then how by the chances and changes of war,
From the time *he* returned, Edward's home lay afar
In the enemy's lines; and the strict, watchful care
Rendered almost impossible intercourse where
Tidings best could be had.   How, despite each endeavor,
Some o'erruling providence still seemed to sever

The long diverged paths, till he feared e'en to greet
A newly-found clue, lest it bring new defeat.
Now that the storm in its fury was spent,
And homes, here and there, welcomed loved ones who went
The tempest to brave, Edward, anxious to end
Forever the doubt 'round the fate of his friend,
And knowing full well to the old village home,
Endeared by his love, if alive, he would come,
Had himself hastened thither. Thank Heaven, his mission
Was crowned with the fullest and grandest fruition!

XI.

ETHRIC.

Aye! our own load of sorrow is lost in the past,
And a radiant future before me is cast;
For the vows, long postponed, shall, I trust, soon be spoken,
And sunbeams are brightest through heavy clouds broken.
But over the land there is echoed a wail,
And its voice unsubdued will through years tell a tale
Of suffering and wrong, and endurance and woe,
That over our history for all time will throw
A terrible shade. True, the question decided,
Heaven once more unites what mankind had divided.
The fiat is spoken, but decades will roll
Ere the task is accomplished. The death-knell must toll
Over deep, lasting prejudice, envy and hate,
And long-abused power. In patience must wait
The land sore oppressed, and the future shall learn
The triumph that right and forbearance must earn.

EDWARD.

The picture you draw, though a dark one, I fear
Will be but repainted by many a year.

Yet, glancing once more o'er the paths we have trod,
And tracing the battles, one sees there a rod
Stretched forth in full power: as Moses laid bare,
Through the wild waste of waters, a broad roadway where
His nation might pass.   For our people have done
Their stern duty well; and our armies have won,
In spite of the dearth of equipments and bread,
Over hosts fully armed, well commanded and fed,
Grand victories that startled the civilized world,
And proved all the zeal and the earnestness hurled
In the terrible strife.   Yet, behold! on the track
Of each grand success stretched the rod, forcing back
The turbulent waters, and leaving a way
For the foemen to pass.   Now the nations obey,
Unconsciously truly, decrees which control
Each destiny singly, thus shaping the whole.
Back through the ages, in harmony wrought,
We may trace saddest histories, each being fraught
With weighty importance.   Thus time will make plain
The ill we have suffered ; and feeling no stain,
No mark of dishonor, the record we leave
As a thread in the loom.   When the long years shall weave
The full pattern out, then its worth being known,
Each consequence wrought by its means will be shown.

XII.

For a moment was silence, as back to the cause
They had lost, memory wandered.

                   Each in the brief pause
Glanced at Edward's loose sleeve, and a tear dimmed his
     eye,
As Ethric said, gently:
                  " 'Twas given to buy

The name that we craved.   Be the sleeve at your side
The badge of your truth and devotion,—your pride.
Be your other arm stronger, throughout life to shield
The dear one whose love may your best blessing yield.
Be your record in future one bright as the past,
From which shall no stain that can tarnish be cast
O'er the truth of that manhood that led you to brave
Fierce dangers your national honor to save.
Your oath is fulfilled.   Let a friend's blessing dwell
O'er your home and your love, wreathing there its bright
     spell,
As a fair, choice garland, whose perfume shall rise
Like clouds of sweet incense that float to the skies.
Be our lives in the future, as true men's lives given,
Full and free each to love, and to country and Heaven !"

His hand Edward grasped as the hand of a brother,
While the fervent " Amen !" passed from one to the other.

CANTO NINETEENTH.

I.

HOMEWARD bound from the orient sailed a ship on,
And it bore to her land, long forsaken, Theon.
Time had dealt kindly with her, for the spring
Of indwelling gentleness ever must bring
Like gentleness 'round one.   That Ethric was dead
Her uncle believed; and his care sought to shed
A light that would break through the clouds of her sorrow,
And teach her young life from its source strength to borrow.
Through respect to her faithful devotion, the truth
He buried in silence, and trusted to youth,
That its buoyancy soon from the dark spell would wake,
And time with its power, and change, yet might break
The strong link that bound her to love and the past,
While pleasure a charm o'er the present would cast.
So he hurried her on o'er the ocean to dwell
Where varying scenes wrought their magical spell.
They roamed o'er the lands where historians trace
Full many a struggle for Fame's highest place.
They passed down the rivers whose long, winding course
Stored wonderful legends of Chivalry's force.
They climbed o'er the Alps, there to bask 'neath the sun
Of Italy's warm, glowing skies.   And yet none
Of strangeness of travel or story o'ercame
Theon's quiet sadness.   That dear, sacred name
Her lips never uttered, yet oft there would come
A craving she could not conceal for her home.

II.

Her uncle had watched her, and, seeing this thought
Was uppermost still, that all others were fraught
With its full, precious burden, had yielded at last,
And turned toward the scenes of the sorrowful past.
Yet e'en to Theon, as she scanned the sad years,
So dark with their shadows, forebodings, and tears,
The weary suspense seemed, alas! but to prove
The tidings that Harold had hurled at her love.
She had written to Edward; but always there came
Kind letters and gentle, yet ever the same
Hope-withering answer, "No more has been heard,"
And a promise to write just as soon as a word
Could be gained in her favor; as yet that was all.
She had heard o'er the seas that the terrible pall
Of suffering and warfare was lifted, and still
Her own cup of sorrow was heaped to the fill.
And the ship travelled on to the land where her woe
Seemed lingering its heavier weight to bestow.

III.

Another ship sped o'er the wave from the West,
And it bore Ethric on, for no moment of rest,
No respite from search could he know till at last
Theon had been found and suspense was all past.
One evening, while listlessly pacing the deck
And watching a sail, which afar off a speck
On the horizon appeared, by the light breeze whirled,
A scrap floated near; for a moment it twirled,
Then fell at his feet, yellow, creased, and old,
And valueless seemed. Half-revealed 'neath the fold

Ethric's quick, startled eye traced the clear-written name
"Clyde Rutherford" there. What it was? Whence it
  came?
These questions impatiently flashed o'er his mind
As the scrap he secured, in amazement to find,
In bold, manly hand, written out on the page
(Well handled, and marked with the impress of age)
The words of the song that had served to recall
His soul from its sorrow that night at the Hall;—
And she who had sung it?

IV.

   A lady sat near
As he turned on the deck, and her eyes, bright and clear,
From her book wandered far, as if waking she dreamed;
Unconscious of others around her she seemed.
For an instant he watched her there, seeking to trace
In his memory what in the pale, troubled face
Seemed dear and familiar. In peaceful repose
Each feature, and yet there were lines to disclose
Suggestions of sadness. Her hair, silvery gray,
Told the tale of the winters she met in life's way.
No others were by. Was this paper her own?
And that melody hers? Could this be the Unknown
Of that memorable night? Undisturbed by the sound
Of his footstep, absorbed in her revery profound,
She moved not, and Ethric the paper retained,
Resolving acquaintance should ere long be gained.

V.

The night gathered 'round, and the steamer ploughed
  through
The darkness that shrouded all else from their view;

The passengers passed from the deck one by one,
And Ethric was left to his musings alone.
Moments sped on, the while fated souls slept,
And stars twinkling o'er them their night vigils kept.
The watcher grew pale as he stood at his post,
And pointed on toward the orient coast,
Where a vessel was seen wrapped in one sheet of fire,
Driving right on their way. And the flames leaping higher
Seethed and hissed in the rigging, and fanned with their
     breath
The travellers they wakened from slumber to death.

VI.

Every nerve then was strained, every man sprang to place,
And the " Antarctic" bounded in furious race
With the danger. The flames in their terrible glow
There pictured out boldly the suffering and woe.
With a glass Ethric stood, and could see women clasp
Their little ones close to meet death's stronger grasp ;
And brave men were struggling their fears to repress,
While the fire-fiend mocked at their helpless distress.

VII.

Soon quick volunteers man the boats. With the first
Ethric springs to his place, while the waves roll and burst,
And so pitiless seem. Is the distance too great ?
Can they reach them with aid ere their terrible fate
May yet be decided ? The burning mast falls !
Ethric scarce dares to breathe, while the leader's loud calls
Of command are quick heeded. On ! on ! with each bound
The steady oars fall with a dull, heavy sound,
Contrasting with wild, piercing shrieks of despair,
And heart-rending cries floating on the hot air.

VIII.

As they draw near the wreck, starting up in affright,
Ethric utters a shriek that rings out on the night
Like a breaking heart's wail.   Is this Hope's cruel mission?
Of all his bright dreams must this be the fruition?
For she is on board,—his life's idol,—Theon!
Play the fierce flames behind her, their hot breath anon
Lifting the hair that in dark masses falls
O'er the pure, snowy dress.   And the fate that appalls
Even stern men around her, arouses no fear,
Awakens no shrinking from death that is near.
With one arm around her, her guardian stands.
On, on speeds the life-boat!   Ring clear the commands!
Rage fiercer the flames, wreathing all, leaping higher!
Fast settles the steamer!   The life-boat comes nigher!
The oars fall faster,—each muscle is strained!
The rescue has reached them! the distance is gained!
But quick leap the flames like some monster in wrath,
Sweeping by every obstacle met in their path.
Ah! their work is well done, for the surging waves roll
O'er the burned vessel buried with many a soul.
And pale faces float like a horrible dream,
While brave men are searching, and bright lanterns gleam.

IX.

Here and there one is saved; now a strong man, who clings
To some frail, broken timber, as last chance that brings
Its sweet hope of life; now a mother, who folds
Her babe in her arms, and herself sinking, holds
Its head above water; perchance now a child
Relentlessly borne on the waves surging wild.

Here and there one is saved; but, alas! deeper down
In the caverns below, while the waves' moanings drown
All cries for assistance, the many must sleep,
And the loved ones at home shall their futile watch keep.
Yet lingers the life-boat; no word has been said.
Each knows there is one not reclaimed from the dead.
See! a maiden floats near with the stiffening arm
Of an old man around her, as if from all harm
E'en in death he would shield her; a deep, gaping wound,
The blow of some spar, on his temple is found.
With a low cry of grief Ethric leaps in the ocean.
The men read the cry; quick the boat is in motion;
And Ethric has lifted her tenderly there,
And then the old man, now unheeding all care.
The boat hurries back with the faint, rescued few,
And the billows roll on, hiding all else from view.

X.

They have come to the ship. Pale, unconscious Theon
Ethric folds in his arms, bears her tenderly on
Past the keen, gazing eyes. And the men whisper low
As the old man is gently laid down. Come and go
Thus the sorrows and pleasures and hopes of this life,
Mingling each with the other.

XI.

         While rumor is rife,
From the now aroused throng comes a lady and gazes
On the face of the dead long and earnestly, raises
One hand to her lips, and quick hurries away
From the crowd to her room, where the first light of day
Faintly enters, that off in this stillness alone
She may weep, undisturbed, for the love she has known;

Bitter tears of regret for the sacred ties broken ;
Bitter tears of remorse for the idle words spoken.

XII.

The vessel sailed on, while the passengers saw
An old man had perished, and gathered with awe
When the body was sunk in the dark, angry wave;
The lady stood with them, and wept o'er his grave.
They thought it a stranger's tears thus kindly given ;
They heard not the heart's cry of anguish to Heaven.

CANTO TWENTIETH.

I.

THEON's wedding evening.   How like some dark dream
The shade from her life that was lifted!   The gleam
Of beautiful sunshine now lovingly shone
Across her smooth pathway, as if to atone
By very intensity of its full light
For clouds and the darkness of vanishing night.

II.

She had roused on the ship as one wakes from a sleep,
With a vague sense of floating afar on the deep,
And of fierce, raging flames.   She had thought it a trance,
When Ethric's own eyes met her swift, eager glance,
Telling hope's sweet fulfilment.   But since she had heard
From Ethric's own lips every quick spoken word
Telling all she would know:—of his capture ; the space
Of long weary weeks, dull and blank, when the race
Of life seemed near finished ; and that peril past,
The struggle of memory returning at last;
Of his letters unanswered ; of months of suspense
That endless appeared, till their burden intense
Could no longer be borne.   Then he hastily told
Of his midnight escape from the Northern stronghold ;
Of his hurrying on to her home but to find
The blight and the havoc that war left behind ;
Of that desolate place, and more desolate room,
All darkened and dismal as some dreary tomb ;

Of the song that had roused him to duty again,
And brought him new purpose, new hope in its strain;
Of the oath he renewed on that night to his land,
To his love, when his honor proved worthy her hand;
Of the duty that summoned him back to his place,
The dangers and hardships increasing to face,
'Mid cheerless surroundings.   Companions of yore
Had fallen in battle; there blessed him no more
The sweet, pleasant memories of one safe at home,
Or glad, loving letters that oft used to come.
Instead, but the dreadful foreboding and pain
That pressed his heart heavy, and racked in his brain,
And made him so desperate through more than a year
Of carnage and suffering and terrible fear,
Ere yet came the great final scene of the war,
Fulfilling his oath to his land; then the star
Of his love led him on. 'And he told how he gained
A clue to her travels, and every nerve strained
To find his lost darling, and lay his true heart
At her feet once again.

III.

Theon turned with a start
As he spoke of the ocean.   Her saddest tears fell
As he tenderly told what he scarce dared to tell.
Then again, how the lady had begged for the sake
Of the dead, and a past love avenged, now to take
A mother's kind care of Clyde Rutherford's ward,
Till life's holiest vows should to Ethric accord
The far higher right to protect and defend,
To shield and to cherish until life should end.
For she was Maud's hostess.   The tale Maud had told
Was the tale of the love crushed and silenced and old,

Which, shrouded in hope that a long life endears,
Clyde Rutherford buried in grave of the years.

IV.

And now in that home that was lavishly decked
With the wealth and the grandeur whose visions had
    wrecked
The one earnest love that a maiden had known,
And fashioned a warm, youthful heart into stone;
From that heart that had learned through experience of
    years,
In the cold school of form, and in longings and tears,
That only one chord gives the answering strain
Which a woman demands, and whose absence is pain;
In that home,—from that heart,—for the sake of one name,
For the sake of the pure, happy love ere yet came
The world's chilling influence, freely was poured
At the feet of Theon all the love that was stored
And stifled in silence.

V.

    Kind, delicate fingers,
Whose light, dainty touch yet caressingly lingers
O'er each flowing fold, have the bridal robe draped,
And the blossoms that caught the pure, fleecy veil shaped;
And the last touch is finished. The lady bends low
And kisses the young, smiling face all aglow
With love's brightest visions, and happy Theon
Marks the look that she gives her, which flitting anon
O'er a face where realities cold shadows cast,
Seems lifting a veil and disclosing the past.
For the smile is the same that Theon can recall
In the portrait long hidden at Rutherford Hall.

VI.

The soft bridal dress and the filmy-like veil
Wrap Theon as a cloud.   And her checks, once so pale,
Now flush like the roses, as burdens all past,
Anxieties over, her one hope at last
Has proven reality.   Mists of her tears
So softly are gathered 'tween her and those years,
That outlines of sorrow, all blunt, are toned down;
The mist forms a halo encircling the crown,
Succeeding the cross that had burdened her life.
Its mission was ended.   The pure name of wife,
The dearest and holiest, would soon be her own.
In humility bending to Heaven's high throne,
She sought there the grace and the strength and the power
To garnish that name with each beautiful flower
That bloomed in the Garden of Love.   She would be
Life's all to her husband.   The great unknown sea
On which their frail barks would be launched, reaches wide,
And ebbing, and surging, and swelling the tide.
Were breakers before them, or waves smooth and clear?
Mortal strength is but weakness, the prize rich and dear.
Hence she earnestly sought for a blessing divine
Their hearts' vows to sanction and round them to shine.
With the whispered " Amen !" trembling yet on her lips,
And its sound in her heart, like the lily that sips
The first morning dew, pure and gentle and fair,
She greeted her lover, awaiting her there.

VII.

The few friends who met by her hostess' desire
Had heard of her life, of the smouldering fire

That burned o'er her pathway; and tear-bedimmed eyes
Watched her entrance, and kindly ears caught her replies.
A quick little shiver while facing the throng,
A little more weight on the arm that was strong
For her gentle weakness; the vows spoken low;
The dear benediction; the thought's rapid flow
On the scenes of the moment; at last it is done:
Two lives are united, two hearts are made one.
Then Lady Glenn greets her with motherly kiss,
And whispers,

        "A life crowned with love's rarest bliss
I crave for my darling."

           The widow's sad heart
Revived in the sunbeams she sought to impart.

CANTO TWENTY-FIRST.

I.

In honored Glenn Castle, where many a charm
Wandered down from the past, as if some tender arm
Encircled the present, Theon, as a guest,
Remained in the fullest enjoyment of rest.
She felt in return for her hostess' kind care
A strong tender love, and sincere wish to share
And lighten the sorrow that o'er her life cast
A shadow that deepened, though borne in the past.

II.

She had told them her story.   'Twas long years ago
She was wooed and was won, and had felt the full glow
Of love first awakened in all its rich beauty ;
But flattering voices had turned her from duty.
Came a memorable night, when the fairest of earth
Were gathered in Rutherford Hall, and light mirth
And festivity reigned.   She was there as a guest,
And *he* praised her that evening, and deemed himself blest.
Little knew he the full, restless light in her eye,
The quick, ringing laugh and the merry reply,
In unnatural excitement concealed the wild fear,
Which almost had crazed her.   The hour drew near ;—
And away from the hall, and away from the sight
Of the gladness therein, through the darkness of night,
She had gone with the new-favored lover, whose name
Had dazzled her heart with its visions of fame.

She had gone from it all, and the few who had known
Her engagement with Clyde understood the low moan
Of his deep, silent anguish. The secret was dead,
And around her loved name was no blight ever shed.
Time passed, and she waked from her dream to behold
That life's greatest treasures are not bought with gold.
Thus waking, she donned all her strength to atone
For the wrong she had done, for which henceforth alone
She must suffer remorse. Every murmur was stilled,
The crushed heart was humbled, with penitence filled.
And her husband had gone to his last, silent rest,
And left her the name of a wife, honored, blest.
Not until then had she dared to return
To the home of her youth, or allow yet to burn
The long-smothered flame. 'Twas Maud's story brought
    up
All the dregs that had sunk in her own bitter cup,
And a sympathy stirred for the young tender heart,
That in innocent truth sought for love's purest part.
She had heard in her loneliness over the wave
A voice that pleaded her power to save,
Till she could not resist it. Unknown, she had sought
The home she had clouded; unknown, she had thought
The past to review, the young love to watch o'er:
And turning again from her dear native shore,
To live out alone, as an exile, old age,
Till death should have finished the last mournful page.
She had wept that she failed. Even then came the hour
When justice appeased, had there thrown in her power
The one sacred pleasure, to bless with her love
Her first lover's darling, and let the last prove
Her full, sincere penitence.

III.

Now Theon felt
Ere she left this kind friend that so tenderly dealt
With her in her sorrow,—whose image could trace
Unmistaken identity with that sweet face
In the old garret found,—'twas her place to restore
The packet and talisman ring that she wore.
From the time it was found in obscurity thrust
That packet had seemed to her care a rich trust.
And through the long years of suspense and of sorrow
She had loved in her loneliness comfort to borrow
By wondering its mysteries. Fancy o'erwrought,
Had brought to her mind, now and then, the strange
        thought,
That the gloom o'er her path, and those secrets concealed
Were so linked together, could they be revealed
Her hope would prove true. Perhaps this was suggested
From the ring,—by that past,—by her present invested
With sweet, tender memories. The old-fashioned seal
In its mute, plaintive way, seemed at once to appeal
To that wonderful awe that is everywhere found
For the presence of death. And if fast iron-bound,
No more safe what it held, in the hands of Theon,
Than simply secured by the wax whereupon
Those words were impressed. In the changes of war,
'Mid its strife and its gloom, and in wand'rings afar
The packet she carried. That night on the ocean,
While backward re-reading the scenes of commotion
That crowded her life, o'er the ring on her finger
Came Memory's tenderest fancies to linger.
" It shall be a talisman, blessing each life,"
Had been Ethric's words. Now, with prophecy rife,

They rose up before her ;—the sealed packet sharing
The hope, if 'twas hope, the despair, if despairing.
With that in her hand she had followed the tale
Woven oft and again, till the vision grew pale,
And confused and all tangled, and sleep had come down
By its magic the weird, flitting fancies to drown.
When wakened at last by the wild cries of " Fire !"
That rang on the night, rising higher and higher,
Till the voice in agony failing to speak,
Only sounded the warning in shriek after shriek,
Her quick startled faculties caught up the chain
Of musing where dropped, and the packet again
Intertwined with her fate. She had seized it in haste,
The one thing to save from that terrible waste.
With ribbon she bound it secure to her side,
To be saved with her life, mayhap found if she died.
And her hope was fulfilled by the fate which revealed
A clue to the secrets so solemnly sealed.

IV.

Its mission accomplished, the ring that she loved
Was slipped from her finger,—for had it not proved
A talisman true ? And the packet, safe found,
Despite the strong waves, to her side firmly bound,
From the case where she kept it was tenderly taken,
That the long buried secrets the present might waken.

V.

Her husband, there waiting, glad welcome extended,
As the broad, winding stairway at last she descended.
In the cool, shaded parlor, where rich curtains drawn
Shut out the bright sunbeams that danced on the lawn,
They met their loved hostess.

18

VI.

LADY GLENN.

      Theon, your bright face,
Whence is banished all paleness, and each ling'ring trace
Of languor and care, will speak well for the clime
Of wide-honored England. Why hasten the time
That again bears you hence?

THEON.

      Not the climate alone,
But the full, lavish kindness around me here thrown
By your bountiful hand, and life's bright hope fulfilled,
Have brought back the roses and anxious cares stilled.
Ever through life will fond memories dwell
Round this beautiful spot, and their sweet voices tell
Of love shown me here. But the time has now come
When duties recall us again to our home.

LADY GLENN.

The strife, true, is ended, but yet there remains
The trace of the conflict that swept o'er your plains;
And many a circumstance waits your return
That will carry you back to the days where must burn
The saddest of memories. Think you 'tis wise
So soon to rewaken those echoed replies?

THEON.

The sorrow is past; recollection but gives
A gratitude greater for pleasure that lives.
May not often those seasons, where centred seem all
The sorrows of life, retain pow'r to recall
Some tender emotion whose influence will bind
Our hearts where the darkest of shadows we find?

VII.

Theon, as she spoke, sought to read the calm face
That looked in her own, and she saw there the trace
Of troubled reflections her question had stirred.
Lady Glenn met her glance, yet she uttered no word;—
But she took Theon's hand, pressed her lips to Theon's
    cheek,
And was turning aside.

THEON.

          Stay! Awhile would I speak
Of your past. Dearest friend, can you pardon the pain
I may give as I turn back the closed leaf again?
In the home of my youth, banished far in the gloom,
And locked in the hush of obscurity's tomb,
Years ago, I discovered an image most fair
Of a maiden as yet unacquainted with care.
Her face looked at me with a full, tender love,
And I read there a tale that my own heart could move.
With the portrait I found this, a gold wedding-ring,
And a packet close sealed, which I felt sure could bring
Its secret to light. I have since seen the smile
That beamed from that image and won me the while;
And it teaches me now that by your hand alone
May this strange seal be broken, its secrets made known.
Other touch would profane. For the sake of the dead,
For the sake of the blessing his love would still shed
Round your heart and your life, in his name I return
These relics whose silence so much bade me learn.

VIII.

Lady Glenn took the packet, her eyes dimmed with tears,
And the ring which recalled the sweet memories of years.

With fingers that trembled the old seal she broke,
Glanced over the letters, and rapidly spoke.

LADY GLENN.

There still is some secret, Theon, my dear child,
Other hand than your own had this motto defiled.
These sealed letters bear your address.   One is torn.
But even its fragments of beauty all shorn
Are carefully kept.   See! this paper signed " Maud !"
Can this be her doing ?

IX.

            Amazed at the fraud,
Theon grasped the packet, and Ethric's face flushed,
While bitter words came ; but his kind hostess hushed
Their sound on his lips.

LADY GLENN.

                'Tis not you, but Maud's life
Must bring retribution.   Those angry words, rife
With cold unforgiveness, will not heal the wound
If a wrong has been done you.   The worst scar is found
Not with you but with Maud.   See, the mute tears are
        pleading
For poor, guilty Maud, while Theon is yet reading
Her letter enclosed.   Let us judgment forbear,
Until we have read what is full written there.

ETHRIC.

Wounded honor is hasty.   That woman could do
A deed so unworthy one scarce believes true,
Maud herself shall bear witness.

THEON.

Come times when one stands
Face to face with some passion revealed, which demands
Control of each action. One's conscience and will
In the life-balance weigh 'gainst that force which, until
The time unsuspected, amassed its full power,
And bursts forth a giant at unheeded hour.
Then, the story oft told, is too sadly repeated;
The good that is in us lies prostrate, defeated;—
Yet subdued cannot die, for its memory lives on,
And bitterly weeps for the one moment gone.
It was so with poor Maud. From her one, earnest love,
All smothered and trampled, arose yet to prove
The life that still lingered, that passion which made
The moment's decision; for suddenly weighed,
Mad jealousy triumphed o'er conscience, and brought
With victory burdens of penitent thought.
For she loved you, my husband. Yet listen! I read:

X.

" Theon! Lives a voice in your heart that can plead
For a woman's great sorrow? Can the love you have won,
By its own proven worth, for the wrong I have done,
Speak a word in defence? Have you known, at the time
When in bitterest scoffing I spoke, rang the chime
Low down in my heart of a requiem sad,
Whose phantom-like knell must have driven me mad
Had it not been thus hushed? Seems it long years ago,—
And yet life is before me, so heavy and slow
Does Time drag his footsteps,—when startled, I heard
The harmony drawn from a newly-swept chord,
And my nature was roused. Was it womanly pride
Or a merciless fate that should evil betide,

Which a fuller test craved?   Alas! had there been given
The proof that was wanted, this earth had been heaven!
Like a cloud-hidden sunbeam, the sweet vision vanished;
That chord from my being forever was banished.
For I tossed the bright bubble of hope in the air,
Then laughed like a child at its sport when the fair,
Glittering plaything had fallen.   What was love then to me
But a memory that wailed ' To have been'?   I was free!
Came a moment at last, when I met face to face
The dream that had vanished.   My fingers could trace
A long, single pathway, that, winding through years,
At last met your own;—and the hushed, latent fears
Had uttered their warning.   Your secret concealed,
My poor, starving heart's intuition revealed.
Impelled by sheer madness, I blindly rushed on,
Having only this thought;—that the hope whereupon
His future was builded should crumble and fall,
And his happiness lie, like my own, 'neath a pall
That time could not lift.   You were young, and the sorrow,
If such it should prove, I had thought some bright morrow
Would speedily heal.   I have seen your pure trust
Living on 'neath the dagger-like strokes that were thrust
At its very foundation.   I have watched your cheek pale,
And have read 'neath your silence the full, plaintive tale
Of a constant endurance that puts me to shame,
And a bright halo sheds around Love's sacred name.
Believe me, Theon, had I pow'r to retract
From all I have done,—could this one fearful act
Whose haunting reproaches have roused me in pain,
Be erased from my life with its terrible stain,
I would willingly turn from my beautiful dream,
And wipe from my memory its last, fading gleam.

A voice of warning has bid me be true,
And urges me now all the wrong to undo.
I will make reparation. Theon, for your sake,
I will meet him again. For your love, I will take
The doubt from your lives, and your full peace restore,
Even though in so doing I open once more
A deep, bleeding wound. And yet, no! 'Tis the last,
Sad, sweet, lingering look I may take of the past.
You will grudge me not this? You have seen the tears
    fall
O'er the face of some dear one that lies 'neath the pall
When the last look is had ere the coffin-lid closes,
And dust with its dust in all silence reposes.
Yet we know that in time, memory clothes with sweet
    grace
The cold, hardened lines of that death-chiselled face,
And its image, though sad, is yet sacredly kept.
Be it thus evermore. O'er my love I have wept;
It has gone from me now. O believe me, Theon!
Though the love of your heart writes its dirge, thereupon
I would not cast a shadow. 'Tis your love has taught
My heart to find rest e'en in penitent thought.
Let me learn from you still. Let your influence hover
Protectingly round me. In this broidered cover,
(A family relic, moth-eaten and worn,
Yet like some old memory the present has shorn
Of happiness, bearing its own cherished spell
That silently seeks of past pleasures to tell,)
I have sacredly, tenderly, guarded for years
A letter I loved. I have shed bitter tears
O'er its pages, and kissed it, then hid it from sight
As a memory that mocked; turning off in affright

From emotions it called.   Now in fragments it lies,
By my own hand destroyed.   Like the hope it defies
I have put it away.   In the day when you read
This page that I write, let its mute fragments plead
For my sore, tempted heart.

   *   *   *   *   *   *   *

                     In the silence of night
(Nature's night and my own,—fitting time,) I must write
The whole story out.   O Theon ! I am crazed,
Hardened, desolate, blind.   All the hope that was raised
Is blighted and mocked by a stern, stubborn fate.
Called forth like the fiend of the past, frenzied hate
Has trodden o'er all, crushing low there forever
Every impulse of good, every honest endeavor
The wrong to atone.   I had meant on the morrow
This package to leave, putting end to your sorrow.
Though confession is sealed, yet I dare not convey
These secrets abroad.   I will hide them from day
And from sight,—hide them far 'mid the years' gathered
     gloom ;
Revealing them, fate shall reveal my heart's doom.
And yet, I foresee, spite of all I have done,
The time when your love shall have full triumph won ;
For Justice, unaided, her ends shall attain,
And Truth regard all that assails with disdain.
In the years that will come, in the sweet years of rest,
When the love of your heart with all blessing is blest
In hope's full fruition, should chance e'er unfold
These far-hidden secrets, turn then, and behold
A heart, young in life, that is seared and has bled ;—
Nay, more,—that though throbbing is withered and dead.
All the secret retain, should you meet in your way,
Pressing on in the throng, steeled, and careless and gay,

That dead-living heart.   What the pleasure or pain
Of one to the world?   What the hope proven vain?
Irresistibly borne, hither, thither one glides,
And the masses pause not for the ill that betides.
Let the past hold its burden.   To you, you alone,
Have I looked for compassion.   Ere justice atone
For the wrong I have done, let some warm, loving word,
Heaven-born in its tenderness, kindly be heard
In your own heart of hearts.   Then perchance may be felt
By me its far influence, and blessing be dealt
To you in rebound; while the angels applaud
A thought drawing earth nearer heavenward.

" MAUD."

XI.

Ethric had picked up the letter whose pieces
Bore true, silent witness of Maud's strange caprices,
And glanced it all over.   The youth's ardent madness,
The fairy-wrought visions, so buoyant in gladness,
To the man, full matured, appeared airy foundation
For love's noble temple.   In mute contemplation,
While his wife was still reading, he turned leaf by leaf
Of the chapter, and traced from the source of Maud's grief
His own lasting happiness.

XII.

ETHRIC.

    Well did the coldness
Which met my appeal picture out in its boldness
The idol I worshipped.   That magical wand
Disrobed it of beauty, and caused it to stand
In truth of its nature.   Not love that I cherished
For the pure and the good, but the idol had perished.

And there stood in its place but a statue despoiled,
Before whose deformities true love recoiled.
That letter has lifted the curtain at last,
Revealing the motives that governed the past.
Yet who could have thought when I bade her " Farewell"
By her summons, her hauteur concealed the deep spell
That influenced her life? Who could hear the fierce
    raging
Of low muffled war that her passions were waging ?

LADY GLENN.

Poor Maud !   How, alas ! has her own mournful story
Robbed youth of its brightness, its peace, and its glory.
For she who in blindness a nurtured hope dashes
On life's barren rocks, will at last find to ashes
Such mockery crumbles.   That woman who spurns
For pride's sake devotion, in dreary years turns
To behold out of reach all the heart longs to cherish,
While reality scoffs at the dreams that must perish.

ETHRIC.

A terrible justice presides over hearts :
Whether trampling one's own or another's fierce darts
Pursue the offender.   The wrong that was done,
And confessed in this packet, its full course has run ;
Now harmless it sinks, and its punishment bears
In the tears it has shed, and dishonor it wears.
In this hour of peace and thanksgiving, Theon,
Let us banish forever the sorrow thereon
That encompassed our lives.   Each bright hope possessing,
Send we now o'er that " dead-living heart" a rich blessing,
Which kindly shall smile on its numbness and dearth,
And waken some purer emotion to birth.

THEON.

Aye, the past shall be dead! Let no harsh echoes mar
The future that cheeringly stretches afar.
To you, my dear friend, need the farewells be spoken
That part us henceforth? Yet, the tie is unbroken,
And the voice is unhushed that has urged your return
To the land of your childhood; for love must still yearn
For long-cherished places. In Rutherford Hall
Your fair, youthful image still hangs on the wall.
Let its smile prove an earnest of peace in that home
Where your age may find rest. Hark! the Past bids you
    " Come!"

ETHRIC.

And the Present re-echoes! Their pledges believe.
Let proven devotion and kindness receive
In sweet benediction, the right you have won
To claim the protection of daughter and son.

XIII.

The shadows were scattered. The full, radiant Crown
Came to age and to youth; and the Crosses laid down
In the past, floating backward, were gilded with love,
Their dark edges softened by light from above.

CANTO TWENTY-SECOND.

I.

THERE are days that are dear to us: Memory clings
Around them with tenderest charm, and oft brings
A flood of pure light to encircle them o'er,—
A halo of happiness dropped from the shore
Of bliss everlasting. Through each hastening year,
That brings to us pleasure or pain, hope or fear,
Increases our love for such days that we know,
That over our lives lasting influence throw.
Perchance, be the memory a sad one, around
Full many a tender, sweet pleasure is found ;
And time, that heals sadness, makes brighter, more fair,
The loved peaceful images clustering there,
Till e'en memories of sorrows have grown so endeared
By wiping them out would the heart be deep seared.
Some days bear a record of pleasure,—not wild,
Impulsive delight,—that is short; but that mild,
And deep-seated happiness, healthy and pure,
Creating bright sunbeams that long shall endure.
These days ever live like the beacon-light's gleam,
That throws o'er the dark waste of waters its beam.
We do well to heed them, for man cannot grow
In genuine strength, if in boasting he throw
Far aside all those tender emotions that dwell
In hearts as yet free from the world's blighting spell.

II.

And such a day comes in our story. The tide
A full year had ebbed and had flowed since, a bride,
Theon with her husband had launched on the main,
While friends lingering near them had echoed again
Their kindliest wishes. And joys were unrolled
As the days flitted by, and sweet pleasures were told ;
For love had grown stronger and holier still,
Its pure gentle presence seemed all things to fill.

III.

Now, once again, ere the story be done,
Return we together, while low sinks the sun,
And casts his long, bright rays aslant o'er the wall
Of that hallowed old homestead, quaint Rutherford Hall.
The acres surrounding bear many a scar,
That silently tells of the havoc of war,
And the fortune their owners could boast years ago
Has melted away like the frost and the snow.
Yet quick, willing hands, and brave, resolute will,
Heeding naught of discouragement, render it still
A dearly loved home. Gently fans the light breeze
This calm, summer twilight around the elm-trees,
While under their shadows, in happy reunion,
Are gathered old friends in that freest communion,
Begotten in years when together they shared
Their sufferings and sorrows, and fierce dangers dared.

IV.

Yonder tall man is Edward. Save loss of his arm,
The struggle has left him no traces of harm.
But the thin chiselled lips have a closer set now,
And a firm purpose rests on the slightly-drawn brow.

19

Near by him is standing his faithful Estelle,
On whose fair golden braids do the last sunbeams dwell
In loving caresses ; the quick-changing light
O'er the slightly-drooped head wreathing coronets bright.

V.

Next, an elderly lady.   The years' tales are told
By the frost-silvered bands that across her brow fold ;
Years of anguish and sorrow, long years full of pain,
Whose sad mem'ries echo their bitter refrain
As they die in the past.   But their chill breath is over,
And happiness, peace, and devotion now hover
In blessing around her.   For Lady Glenn lives
In the genial warmth sweetest gratitude gives.

VI.

Theon is the same,—ever gentle and pure ;
The love that she cherished and anchored secure,
Through long years of trial has wrought its full spell,
And wakened new graces around it to dwell.
Her husband receives it as some priceless gem,
Some glorious treasure whose rich diadem
Shall crown his whole life with a blessing untold ;
And his manhood grows stronger that love to uphold.

VII.

This day, that has finished their first married year,
To all has been crowded with memories dear.
For to-day many gathered in yon silent city,
And brought, for the sake of their love and their pity,
Fair flowers to wreathe over each honored grave
Where rests in deep slumber who perished to save
The sacred " Lost Cause."   As they slowly passed on,
Decking graves where were heroes reposing, Theon

Read a name on the marble whose memories back
Led her mind through the years of her sorrow's dark track.
For Harold slept there, and the past was forgiven,
And the happy wife wept for the fate that had driven
A wild, selfish will madly on in the strife,
Till it proved the great wreck of an uncontrolled life.

VIII.

Lived the past in the day.   Loving thoughts of the dead
Were wakened again.   There were secret tears shed
For homes that were broken, and hopes that were buried,
And dear ones that forth to the battle were hurried;—
For the Land where the Cypress was twined with the glory;—
For the deeds that were written in characters gory.
And now they had gathered to talk it all over,
While memory seemed with new fondness to hover
'Round each thrilling scene;—and their voices were low
And trembled while telling of days of their woe.

IX.

While the sun was just sinking they wandered apart,
As if in the silence of evening each heart
Sought its thought and repose.   Ethric there, and Theon,
Took the old trodden path 'neath the elm-trees, whereon
The soft breezes played.   Up and down while they talk,
In their long, sheltering shadows they saunter.   The walk
Is a happy one now, and unlike the slow tread,
And quick, watching ear, and the low, drooping head
Which marked Theon's carriage when meeting her woe
Underneath the same elm-trees but four years ago.
Ethric around his wife's neck has just placed
A chain, with a cross, upon which there is traced
A circlet of leaves;—and a sweet tale is told
By the letters there daintily traced on the gold.

One side bears the date of their joy and " Theon ;"—
The other, the circlet inclosing thereon
The sweet, cheering motto, " No Cross," then, " No Crown."

X.

What gift more appropriate?   Now far adown
The vista of years has receded their cross,
So hard and so heavy to bear.   At its loss
The bright crown appears, and 'tis brighter by far
Because of the weight of the cross.   Every scar
That burden had left them has happiness healed :
The strength that it gave them each life has revealed.
And now heart in heart, hand in hand they look back
To scan once again the old time-beaten track :
Turning thence to the present, where banished all gloom,
Secure they repose in the old happy home.
Life appears beautiful, bright, and serene ;
And, trusting, they face all the future unseen.
Experience has taught them each happiness here
Must walk hand in hand with some shadow or tear.
By Infinite Wisdom is each life controlled,
And shadow or sunshine to each is unrolled,
As each is most needed.
               Then Ethric bends down,
And tenderly says,
               " Here the Cross, there the Crown !
God grant that to each of us grace may be given
The Cross to bear here, and the Crown wear in heaven !"

THE END.